As a brown bear who's been be-spelled by witches and rescued by horsemen and demons, Madagascar has spent
months recovering. He's bored. When Kontra's gang gathers
the information they need to take out a facility holding and
experimenting on shifters, he decides to help them. While
there, Madagascar runs across his mate—a wolf shifter working as a janitor . . . who pulls a gun on them. After disarming
and securing the man, they learn his name is Ishmael Cartwright, a shifter who'd been kidnapped and sold by a now-
deceased councilman gone rogue. The experiments done on
Ishmael have left him with little memory of his past, and he
believes any recollections of him shifting are delusions
brought on by the house fire that left scars on his back. With
Ishmael believing the scientists saved him, can Madagascar
find some way to break through his conditioning and win his
mate?

Reconditioning the Wolf
Copyright © 2023 Charlie Richards
ISBN: 978-1-4874-4000-8
Cover art by Angela Waters

Published by eXtasy Books Inc

Look for us online at:
www.eXtasybooks.com

Reconditioning the Wolf
Kontra's Menagerie 36

By

Charlie Richards

DEDICATION

In family life, love is the oil that eases friction, the cement that binds closer together, and the music that brings harmony.
~Friedrich Nietzsche

CHAPTER ONE

"You're going to do what?"

Madagascar had expected his older brother's shocked question upon his announcement. "I'm going to go with Kontra and some of his people to shut down the facility they've been researching," he repeated.

Congo scrubbed a hand through his thick dark hair. "Yeah, that's what I thought you said," he rumbled, concern evident in his voice, scent, and expression. "But . . . why?" Congo asked with a shake of his head.

With a shrug, Madagascar tried to put into words what he was feeling, and he couldn't very well just tell his brother that he was bored. "I feel like . . . I should be doing something," Madagascar began slowly, trying to explain. Just because he'd anticipated Congo's incredulity didn't mean he'd had a proper response prepared beforehand. "Something to . . . I don't know, help others after so many have helped us."

Maybe there was something to Congo's assertions that Madagascar didn't always think before he acted. Even after over two years under the spells of a circle of witches, being trapped in his brown bear form and forced to do their bidding for fear of bone-deep pain debilitating him, that didn't seem to have changed. On the other hand, perhaps that had just exacerbated Madagascar's tendency. Since he could once again act on his own inclinations, he wanted to exert his control in every way possible.

When Congo sighed deeply, rested his hand on Madagascar's shoulder, and squeezed lightly while smiling,

1

Madagascar realized he must have said something right.

"I understand," Congo told him, his deep voice soft and low. His brother smiled warmly at him. "I'm proud of you for wanting to pass it on."

Madagascar sucked in a sharp breath. His bear rumbled happily within his mind. His chest warmed upon hearing his brother's praise. Not only was Congo his older brother, but the man was the Alpha of their brown bear shifter sleuth — as small as it was with only six members remaining.

Eight now, if we count the couple of mates Congo and Shannon found and bonded with.

And I do not feel jealous. Nope, not one bit.

"I know I don't say it enough, Mads," Congo muttered, using his other arm to pull him into a hug. "But I am proud of you. After everything we've endured, we deserve to not only build a new life, but to be happy." While nuzzling Madagascar's temple with his goatee, Congo murmured, "If going on this expedition makes you happy, then you have my blessing." Drawing away, Congo pinned him with a serious expression. "Just be careful. Okay? You're the only family I got."

Madagascar decided not to correct Congo's assumption of why he'd fallen silent. No way did he want his brother to know about his discontent at not having found his own special someone. He just had to keep believing that Fate would smile upon him one day.

Plus, technically, Madagascar wasn't the only family he and Congo had left. They had two other brothers. Somewhere out there was their eldest brother, Kenya, as well as their youngest brother, Chad. When he and Congo had left their sleuth due to being gay, the pair had joined the rest of the sleuth in turning their backs on them.

Some nights, Madagascar lay awake in bed and wondered if the pair ever thought of them — ever wondered where they were and if they were safe. On more than one occasion, he'd been tempted to ask Lamar — a tech-savvy peacock shifter in

Kontra's gang—to look into them. So far, Madagascar had resisted, too afraid of what he might find.

Focusing on Congo, Madagascar offered a small nod and a cocky grin. "I'll be fine, big bro. Don't you worry." He squeezed his brother's upper arms, offering comfort. "You know these guys know what they're doing." Barking a laugh, Madagascar added, "Besides, I'm teamed up with Beta Sam and his mate Ryan. The dude's enhanced. Did you know that?"

"Enhanced?" Congo appeared confused. "What's that mean?"

Over the course of the year, Madagascar and the other bears in Congo's sleuth had been recovering from the witches' spells. The bitches had carved them into the backs of their skin in a ritual using demon blood, stripping them of free will and forcing them to follow the orders of magick users. Although, the occasional dominant paranormal, like Kontra, as well as the Four Horsemen of the Apocalypse who'd rescued them, could get them to respond, too. Meeting those guys had been super cool in a really scary way.

During that time, Madagascar had heard stories from many of the guys about how they'd met their mates.

"Well, Ryan was a soldier, a sniper," Madagascar explained. "And one of his commanding officers approached him about getting his abilities enhanced." With a curl of his lip, he rumbled, "Guess some military stooges were working with some of the scientists and getting some of their best to agree to experimentation by showing them bogus propaganda videos about paranormals attacking humans." Crossing his arms over his chest, Madagascar shrugged. "Anyway, Ryan got his eyesight and reflexes enhanced before he'd discovered the truth and started helping shifters. That's how he met Sam. A wolf pack sent him up to Kontra's people to give them a hand." Recalling their story, Madagascar smiled wistfully. "They had a few bumps, but they got together, and the rest, as they say, is history."

"Huh." Congo chuckled softly, shaking his head. "Guess I've been a little wrapped up in my mate's activities to have heard."

Madagascar nodded. He knew that Congo's panda bear shifter mate, Zhaul, was working with the group trying to get a few of the more stubborn or abused shifters to change into human form. There were also several who'd been experimented on, and with the drugs involved, Eli—Kontra's pack doctor—had been working long-distance with a doctor in a wolf shifter pack to figure out what was in their system and clear it so they could shift, too.

Last Madagascar had heard, there were a number who couldn't—or wouldn't—change. There was a trio that had been held by a different group of witches than their bear sleuth in a sort of animal refuge that they used to make money—a gray wolf, a capybara, and a coral snake. The elephant and camel who'd been with them had shifted upon finding their mates, so everyone had hope that it would happen that way for them, too.

Another group in Kontra's people's care had been at another scientist facility that they'd taken out just prior to Madagascar's arrival. Zhaul had come from that group. Although he'd been able to shift shortly prior to their arrival—as had Able, a leopard shifter who'd mated with Olson, the owner of the Victorian home they were staying at in the bayou—several others were taking longer.

A meerkat named Mickey had recently begun to shift just prior to meeting his mate—CIA Agent Rhone Craigson—and he'd left with Rhone the week before. After a close call, the agent had discovered who'd been leaking information to the military. Rhone had needed to return to help his boss end that source, and as his mate, Mickey had insisted on being by his side.

There was a rhino from that group, too, and Madagascar had learned that he'd shifted just the previous day. His name was Aaron, and he didn't stay in human form for long stretches, yet. The last two were a vulture and a sloth, and neither had been seen shifting so far.

"Well, again, be careful, Mads," Congo encouraged, patting Madagascar on his shoulder again. "Accidents can happen even with the most well-thought-out plans."

Madagascar would never say it, but he appreciated that Congo still worried for him, even though they were both well over a hundred years old. "I will," he promised.

Best laid plans of mice and men, and all that.

After squeezing Madagascar's neck once, Congo released him and stepped back. "It'll be morbidly interesting to see what you all find this time," he grumbled with a shake of his head. Then Congo turned and headed toward the back of the house.

Madagascar silently agreed as he headed in the other direction.

Stepping into the front yard, Madagascar paused and swept his gaze over the myriad of men preparing to leave. Kontra's people loaded two SUVs and two box trucks with supplies. Their expressions were a mixture of anticipation, concern, and determination. Except for Payson—a hyena shifter that Madagascar knew he wasn't alone in thinking had a few screws loose. No, Payson grinned widely and rushed about in obvious glee. Payson's human mate, Land, however, stood on the front porch with a mixture of worry and fondness on his face.

"You ready?" Sam asked, the big Texas-longhorn bull's long legs quickly closing the distance between them. "Get permission from your brother?"

While Madagascar hadn't realized that was what he was doing, Beta Sam was right. His brother was his alpha. He

5

hadn't truly *needed* it to go, but he'd wanted it.

"Yes, sir," Madagascar replied.

Sam tipped his chin in a small nod before turning and leading the way toward one of the SUVs.

Madagascar slipped into a middle captain's chair, his excitement ramping up.

It took every ounce of self-control Madagascar felt to keep from bouncing on his toes. He hadn't told Congo, but Ryan had given him several shooting lessons. Even though Madagascar wouldn't call himself a marksman, yet, he wouldn't shoot any of his own people, either.

Plus, Madagascar would be more liable to shift into his bear if any real problems started.

Or I'll stay back with Lamar, covering the peacock shifter, like Kontra and Sam instructed.

Sam, Ryan, Lamar, and Rueben — Lamar's human mate — were headed to the control room. Madagascar was going with them. They were supposed to keep Lamar safe as he took control of their systems.

Of course, Madagascar had heard that Lamar was no slouch at taking care of himself. The shifter appeared fastidious and uptight, considering the way he always appeared clean and put together. Only his rough and tumble human mate managed to ruffle his feathers, and Lamar seemed happy about that.

"Remember," Sam reiterated, focusing on Madagascar. "Stick with the group. No one goes off alone."

"Yes, Beta," Madagascar confirmed, even though that had to have been the tenth time Sam had said that.

A second later, Madagascar knew he wasn't the only one to hear Kontra's deep voice ordering that they advance through his earpiece.

Sam hefted a firearm in his right hand and the forged keycard in his left and led the way toward the secluded warehouse-like building hidden deep in the swamp. They'd already bypassed a security fence and a number of cameras. They'd just been waiting for all the other groups to get into position.

Madagascar's group was going through what was supposed to be a secret entrance closest to the control room. There was a guard room they would need to neutralize outside it. The barracks were on the other side of the building, so most of Kontra's people would be going in on that side.

Hoping their small incursion could swiftly and quietly secure the room, Madagascar followed the others through the swamp.

After Sam swiped the card through the reader, the door beeped. Rueben opened the door. Ryan slipped through the opening, his rifle ready at his shoulder. Sam followed his mate.

As ordered, Madagascar hurried after them, Lamar flanking him. He heard the door click behind him and knew that Rueben was at their back. They paused at a door to the left, and after Sam opened it, Ryan confirmed that it was clear.

Madagascar had been told that the word meant the room was empty.

They passed two more empty rooms without incident. Evidently, entering at night had been a good idea. Supposedly, that meant there would be little staff on hand, so fewer people to raise the alarm.

Just as they reached the door with a plaque heralding *Control Room, Authorized Personnel Only*, a high-pitched claxon sounded through the place.

The alarm.

Madagascar couldn't help wincing upon hearing the offending noise, but the others didn't react. Instead, Sam used his keycard to try to unlock the door. It worked, the light on the panel turning green.

Rueben yanked open the door, and Ryan swung into the

opening, weapon at the ready.

Able to see over Ryan's shoulder, Madagascar made out two occupants—a slender guy in white sitting at a control panel and a huge, black-haired guy standing next to a bucket holding a mop. Unable to help himself, Madagascar found himself admiring the clearly shocked janitor's heavily muscled body and lightly bronzed skin. His black brows had disappeared beneath his shaggy bangs, and his equally dark eyes were huge in his ruggedly handsome face. Even his full lips were parted, and Madagascar found himself wondering what they would taste like.

Shit! Focus!

Without turning from the computers, the slender guy asked, "Well? What triggered the alarm? I'm flipping through the damn screens as fast as I can, but there's too many of the damn things." The human continued to grouse as he kept hitting buttons.

"We're here to shut you down," Ryan replied coldly.

As the computer guy spun in his chair, gasping as he did so, the janitor dropped his mop. He reached into a pouch attached to his bucket cart. A second later, the man yanked out a gun and began lifting it, clearly intending to point it at them.

Ryan squeezed off a round, hitting the panel directly to the left of the janitor's head. "Don't even think about it," he ordered.

The man's fear must have intensified his scent, for it wafted over Madagascar's senses. "Fuck," he whispered, his bear roaring in his mind. *Mine!* "Please don't hurt him."

While Ryan didn't lower his rifle, he commented, "If he continues to lift that gun, I won't have a choice."

At the same time, Sam asked, "Why?"

Staring in shock at the huge man before him, Madagascar whispered in a strained voice, "He's my mate."

CHAPTER TWO

Ishmael didn't know who the guys were or what they were doing there. The fact that they had guns and talked about shutting down the facility meant one thing, though. The men were bad guys—people averse to scientific advancement or environmental terrorists or some shit.

The people who'd saved Ishmael had warned him about such people—namely, Doctor Kaylie Meyer. She'd helped him so much. That was why she and the others working there had trained him on how to use a weapon. Everyone who lived and worked there had to be able to defend themselves at all times from people like these men.

I was too slow to respond. What do I do now?

Guilt flooded Ishmael, and he felt like a big fat failure. He'd failed those who'd saved his life, who'd helped him relearn everything, who'd given him a purpose. These men obviously wanted to stop the good work Doctor Meyer was trying to do, and he should have found a way to stop them.

Of course, there were more of them than me, and Simon is zero help.

A fresh wash of guilt flooded Ishmael upon his uncharitable thoughts. Sure, Simon was a total dick, but he was super smart, too. He was way smarter than Ishmael. Simon manned the computers, and Ishmael cleaned . . . things.

"Put the gun down, buddy, and we won't hurt you."

Snapping his attention to where it needed to be—namely, the guys who'd slipped into the control room while he'd been deep in thought—Ishmael nearly jerked the gun up on instinct. There were five men standing just inside the door. Two of them were really big, two medium, and then one little guy.

All of them were armed. Two were pointing their weapons at Simon, who had his hands raised in the air as if that would help. The first guy still had his rifle pointed at him, while a big guy with a scar had his gun pointed at the floor.

The last man caught Ishmael's eye . . . and not because he had a gun pointed at him. Instead, it was because he had his hands raised in placation and was easing around the side of the room, out from behind the others. Ishmael also thought he was damn gorgeous.

The guy had deep brown skin and warm, dark-brown eyes. His goatee accentuated his strong cheekbones, and there was the smallest of smiles curving his full lips. The black shirt he wore seemed to stretch across his broad chest, accentuating his well-muscled torso.

"Can you put that down for me, man?"

The soft deep voice came from the dreamboat, and Ishmael snapped his attention back to the man's eyes. The man really did have the most gorgeous eyes — warm and friendly with a hint of something else there. Ishmael figured he just might be able to stare into them all day.

"Please, handsome?" The man sounded so entreating. "Can you do that for me?"

Do what?

I wanna do anything for you . . .

Wait. Did he call me handsome? Naw . . . that would be weird. Guys callin' other guys handsome. Except —

"Please, big guy?" The handsome guy sounded so coaxing. "I don't want to see you hurt." To Ishmael, he actually sounded pained as he spoke. "But these guys really gotta secure this room. Ya know?"

Ishmael didn't know, and he didn't really understand. That didn't stop him from slowly lowering his gun as he responded to the gorgeous man's urgings. Plus, Ishmael couldn't think of a damn thing he could do against five men.

Simon doesn't count.

"No, damn it," Simon shouted. "Shoot them!"

Ishmael froze with his gun hovering over the floor.

Maybe I should try?

Acting on the order of one of the workers, Ishmael began to lift his gun again.

"Sorry, man."

Ishmael heard the words right before the ring of a gunshot flooded his ear. That was followed by a burst of pain in his arm—the one holding the gun—and the momentum swung him around. Ishmael's hand slapped into a nearby console, and his fingers twitched, allowing the gun to slip from his fingers.

Oh no.

"Easy!" The handsome man was by his side and gripping his shoulders. "Just lie back."

His dark eyes appeared so worried . . . but why? He was a bad guy, right?

"It's just a flesh wound," the man told him. Then he frowned and scowled over his shoulder. "It's just a damn flesh wound. Right, Ryan?"

"Yeah," the original guy who'd entered with the big-ass rifle claimed. "In and out. Through and through. As soon as you claim the human, he'll be good as new in no time."

The handsome man nodded even as he returned his attention to Ishmael. "Hear that?" he crooned, helping him ease to his back. "You'll be good as new soon enough. You'll—" The man paused, his hands still on Ishmael's upper arms as he half levered over him. His nostrils flared. "What the hell?"

Before Ishmael could even hope to understand what the stranger was talking about . . . at all . . . he moved a hand to the wound on Ishmael's arm. He touched his fingertips to it, wiping up some of the blood. To Ishmael's continued shock, the man lifted it to his mouth, stuck out his tongue, and swiped up the dollop.

"Y-You shouldn't—" Ishmael began. After all, one of the first rules Doctor Meyer had explained to him was the toxicity of blood.

People should never ever *ever* ingest blood.

"Holy shit." The man sounded shocked, his eyes widening. He glanced around the room before snapping his attention to Ishmael. "Y-Y-You're one of us?" Shaking his head, he stared at him in disbelief. "Then why are you helping them?"

"What are you talking about, Madagascar?" The guy who'd been holding the rifle on Ishmael appeared next to the handsome guy's shoulder. "What do you mean by *one of us?*"

Madagascar glanced over his shoulder at the rifleman. Hell, he couldn't have been talking about anyone else. Even Ishmael, with his slow brain, realized that.

"He's a shifter," Madagascar proclaimed before turning his focus back on Ishmael. "Although I'm not certain what kind." The man glanced at Simon for a second before once again staring at Ishmael. "Uh, what are you? And why are you helping them?"

Even though Ishmael really liked the way Madagascar was looking at him, as if he were something special—*which I'm totally not*—he shook his head. "I don't know what you're talking about." Gripping his injured arm just under the wound, Ishmael cringed when Madagascar's brows furrowed, making him look upset. "I'm not a terrorist like you." Ishmael glanced toward Simon, seeing a look of disgust on his face. "I'm really not."

Simon sneered and opened his mouth. "You're such a moron," he muttered before focusing on the smallest man in the group. "Hey, get away from there." Simon even began to rise as if to stop him from whatever he was doing at a nearby computer console.

A big redhead grabbed Simon. "Uh-uh," he stated with a shake of his head. In short order, he flipped Simon around, pulled a pair of cuffs from a pocket, and snapped them around Simon's wrists.

"You bastards," Simon roared, wriggling in his grip. "You're all abominations. We're gonna wipe all free shifters from the map." He sounded like he was ranting, but Ishmael didn't understand what it was about as Simon continued, "The only good shifter is one in a lab, getting used to make humanity better. We'll—"

"And that's enough out of you," the biggest one with a scar grumbled, shoving a gag in Simon's mouth.

"Let's get this cleaned up and bandaged, man," the guy who'd shot him stated, having set his weapon aside. He pulled out some stuff from one of the many pockets in his pants. "Can you watch the door, Sam?"

"We got you covered," the small one claimed, while pointing to a set of monitors. "I'll put the corridors leading to here on those."

"Good, Lamar," the scarred one—Sam—stated. After a glance toward the man holding him, he returned his focus to the indicated monitors. "You sure, Madagascar?"

The gorgeous man—Madagascar—nodded. "Positive." He squeezed Ishmael's hand—the one on his injured arm. "Let go of your arm, my mate. Ryan will get that patched up."

When did he take my hand?

Even as Ishmael flinched away from Ryan, he nibbled his bottom lip as he nodded. "O-Okay." It did really hurt, after all. "If this is what getting shot feels like, I'm glad I don't remember my time in the fire."

"When were you in a fire?" Madagascar asked softly, drawing Ishmael's focus away from where Ryan was cutting away the sleeve of his shirt. "Was it recent?"

"D-Did I say that out loud?" Ishmael muttered. When Madagascar nodded, he flinched. "S-Sorry."

Madagascar squeezed Ishmael's hand again and gave him a reassuring smile. "You don't need to apologize to me," he told him, surprising Ishmael. "I can't wait to learn all about you." Even giving him a smile, Madagascar asked, "What's your name, my mate?"

"Um, Ishmael," he replied, wincing as a fresh stab of pain coursed up his arm. "Ishmael Cartwright." When Simon rolled his eyes, even managing to sneer around his gag, Ishmael muttered, "Maybe I wasn't supposed to tell you."

"It's really nice to meet you, Ishmael," Madagascar claimed, giving him another reassuring smile. "I've been waiting to meet you for a really long time."

"Why?" Ishmael asked, feeling more and more confused by the second. He really liked the sound of Madagascar's deep voice and wanted him to keep talking. "How long?" Being confused wasn't a new thing for Ishmael, but something about what was going on seemed super important to him. "Why are you being nice to me?" Cocking his head, Ishmael blurted out, "You're the bad guys."

"Uh, we're really not," Ryan claimed from where he squatted next to him. He flashed a smile up at Ishmael before returning his attention to where he was bandaging his arm. "I was right where you are not too long ago," he told him. "Confused and fighting for the wrong side." With a pat on Ishmael's shoulder, Ryan straightened. "There. With your shifter healing, you'll be good as new in a few days." He began putting away his supplies as he stated, "We'll explain everything and help you get up to speed on what's really going on."

Simon tried to snarl something, but the gag muffled his words.

"Um, okay," Ishmael mumbled.

Maybe if I play along, they'll let me go. Then I can text Doctor Meyer and tell her what's going on here. She'll be so mad.

"I'm Madagascar, by the way," the handsome black man told Ishmael, confirming his name. "And to answer your question, I'm one-hundred-twenty-three years old." His smile widened. "So I've been looking for you for about a hundred years or so," he claimed with a wink.

"Naw. You can't be that old," Ishmael countered, shaking his head. "You gotta be joshin' me." With a laugh, surprised to find levity in such a scary situation, he told him, "You don't look more than thirty-five. And no one lives that long."

"Shifters do," Madagascar claimed, squeezing his hand again. His expression turned troubled. "Were you raised by humans, Ishmael?"

Ishmael shrugged. "I don't know. I don't remember much from before the fire."

"How long ago was that?" Madagascar pressed.

"Not sure," Ishmael admitted. Seeing Madagascar's concerned look, he hunched his shoulder and muttered, "Um, Doctor Meyer said it was over ten years ago now, but I was in a coma for a while, too."

"Doctor Meyer?" Madagascar pressed.

Simon roared from behind his gag even as he tried to rise from where the redhead had pushed him to the floor.

The redhead stopped Simon from moving, but Ishmael understood anyway.

Tugging his hand free of Madagascar's, Ishmael pulled his knees to his chest and wrapped his arms around them. "I'm not answerin' no more."

CHAPTER THREE

Madagascar wanted to pull Ishmael's hand back into his own. While he desperately wanted to soothe the hulking mountain of a man that was his mate, he knew his touch was no longer welcome — at least, not right then. Plus, Madagascar hated to think it, but he had a niggling idea that his mate was a little on the slow side.

I need to get him away from these scientists and doctors and their influence.

But how to do that without making him a prisoner?

Damn it. I may need to make him a sort of hostage for a bit so I can get everything straightened out with him. He's a shifter, and he's an adult, so why doesn't he know about shifting?

What the hell have the scientists done to him?

Madagascar wasn't stupid enough to think that Ishmael would stay with him by choice, yet. The man didn't know he was a shifter, and he didn't seem to know anything about them. As much as Madagascar wanted to make Ishmael happy, he had a funny feeling that what he would need to do to educate the man would hurt him first.

Damn.

Deciding the best course of action was to let Ishmael rest, Madagascar offered him a small smile. "Okay, Ishmael," he rumbled softly. He squeezed his mate's huge boulder of a shoulder, unable to help his continued desire to touch his mate. Releasing him was the hardest thing he'd ever done. "Just rest and relax."

Madagascar forced himself to turn away from Ishmael.

Moving to Sam's side, he muttered, "What do you think?"

"I think you're in a difficult situation," Sam answered just as softly. He flicked his gaze to Ishmael for a second, then glanced at the monitors before focusing his dark eyes on Madagascar. "We'll get him to the doc and draw his blood, but I don't know what he'll be able to do here in the bayou." After a second of hesitation, Sam muttered, "It just may be time to leave this area."

"Leave the area?" Madagascar couldn't help the surprise in his tone. "What about those who can't shift?" Just as quickly, he offered, "I could drive a box truck."

Sam nodded once. "We could go that route, and we still may." With his attention back on the monitors, he muttered, "But Kontra and a few of us have been discussing other options."

Madagascar wanted to ask what options, but Rueben growled, "Fuck. Who the hell are you contacting, Ishmael?" As he spoke, the bonded human stalked the few steps to Ishmael's side.

Seeing what Rueben had noticed, Madagascar winced. Ishmael had his arms tucked between his knees and his chest, and he was focused on the device he was tapping on. Guilt filling him, he realized he should have been watching his mate.

Rueben reached down and swiped the device, causing Ishmael to cringe and lean away from the clearly annoyed man.

Cursing under his breath, Madagascar rushed to Ishmael's side. Irritation mixed with his guilt, and he bit back his desire to snap at Rueben for scaring his mate. He knew the man wouldn't really hurt Ishmael, and the fact that Ishmael was contacting someone was Madagascar's own damn fault.

I should have been more attentive.

"You're okay, Ish," Madagascar reassured, resting his hand on his shoulder. "Rueben won't hurt you. You just —"

Madagascar bit off his words when a blush filled Ishmael's

cheeks, and he peered at Madagascar from beneath his lashes. The man was just so damn . . . cute. He wanted to kneel next to him and kiss the heat from the man's face, giving him a different reason to flush.

"Who was he contacting?" Sam asked.

"A Doctor Kaylie Meyer," Rueben reported, his attention on the device. "He told her that there are people here with guns who took over the control room while he was cleaning." Smirking, Rueben glanced Ishmael's way. "You must type fast, man." Then he held up the phone for Sam to see and stated, "She told him to keep quiet, listen to our conversations, and let her know if we mention anything odd." With a wide grin and a scoff, Rueben finished, "Like creatures of myths."

"Well, we can be sure that Kaylie knows about us." Sam's expression grew serious. "Is there an address listed in her contact info?"

After a few seconds of typing on the phone, Rueben shook his head. "Afraid not."

"Give it here." Lamar held up his hand. "I'll see if I can trace the signal to where she is."

Rueben handed over the phone as Ishmael issued a soft cry of dismay. The noise tore at Madagascar's heart, and he wished there was some way he could soothe him. Unfortunately, nothing came to mind.

Perhaps also attracted by the noise, Sam focused on Ishmael. "It's commendable that you warned one of the scientists of what's happening here," he stated softly, his tone almost kind. "It shows your loyalty." Sam shook his head once as he rested his hand on Ishmael's opposite shoulder. "I know you don't understand right now, but you've given your loyalty to the wrong people."

Ishmael glanced between them for a few seconds before lowering his gaze back to his knees.

Sam moved back toward the monitors, patting Madagascar's upper back as he passed. "We have company coming," he warned, pulling his gun from his holster. "Hmmm, a team of eight creeping toward us from the direction of the exit."

"Maybe they were sent in response to Ish's message," Ryan proposed, slinging his rifle over his shoulder before drawing his own handgun.

"Could be, but I don't feel like asking," Sam told them. "If they fire, return it."

Upon hearing that order, Madagascar noticed Ishmael press his forehead to his knees and a tremble worked through the man. He couldn't resist placing his hand on his mate's shoulder, hoping to comfort him. Ishmael tensed under his palm for a heartbeat before relaxing again, even going so far as to lean toward him a smidge.

Madagascar felt his bear rumble with pleasure in his mind, pleased with the connection.

"Ah, here comes Kontra's team," Lamar stated, pointing to a different monitor. "He'll take care of them."

Even with the door closed, the sound of gunfire mixed with roars and screams filtered to them. Madagascar heard Ishmael whimper again, confirming his belief that his mate might be huge, but he had a gentle soul. Needing to help Ishmael in some way, he lowered to one knee beside him.

Threading his fingers through Ishmael's thick, black hair, Madagascar leaned close and murmured, "This wasn't your fault." When Ishmael's black-eyed-gaze met Madagascar's own, he saw the sadness within their depths as well as a healthy dose of disbelief. "Whoever sent those soldiers here is at fault," he told his mate. "And unless they were sitting around in the bayou close by, there wasn't enough time between your text and now for the doc to have sent them."

"Mads is right, man," Rueben assured, giving Ishmael a smile. "These guys were probably sent due to the alarm having been sounded." His expression turned grave. "And I know you don't understand right now, but we are at war." After a second, Rueben added, "And we're the good guys."

Madagascar could scent Ishmael's disbelief.

A knock sounded on the door.

"It's Kontra," Lamar announced.

Sam lifted his card to the reader. After the light turned green, he pulled the door open. The alpha stood in the doorway, naked as the day he was born, telling Madagascar that, at some point, he'd chosen to shift.

Kontra glanced around the room, his brow arching when he took in the two prisoners. "Someone want to tell me what's going on?"

"That asshole knows about shifters," Sam stated, indicating the bound and gagged man. Using a thumb, he pointed over his shoulder at Ishmael. "That's Ishmael. He's a shifter in service to the scientists . . . and he's Mads's mate."

"Not a shifter," Ishmael countered, his deep voice soft and low. "No such things."

"Your mate?" Kontra pinned his gaze on Madagascar.

Madagascar nodded. "Yeah."

Kontra rubbed his hand over his goatee. "Well, shit."

Cringing, Madagascar nodded. Even though finding his fated mate was a gift, he worried about Ishmael's state of mind, too. He needed to find a way to get Ishmael talking again.

"And congratulations," Kontra added with a smile. "We'll help you figure this out."

"Why are you naked?" Ishmael asked, looking confused even as he blushed again.

Payson sauntered into the room, also nude. "Cause shifting is hard on the threads," he stated bluntly. Stopping near Ishmael, he crouched next to him and inhaled deeply. "Huh," Payson grunted, only to lean closer and take another deep sniff of Ishmael.

"Payson?" Madagascar clenched his free hand, barely resisting pulling the shifter enforcer away from his mate. "Uh, what are you doing?"

"Scenting him," Payson replied with a *duh* look on his face before looking over his shoulder at Kontra. "His scent is tainted by some chemical."

Kontra hummed deeply in his chest, his eyes narrowing.

Madagascar winced as he refocused on Ishmael. "You're taking pills for something?" He recalled then that Payson had the best nose of anyone. It suddenly clicked, and a gasp escaped him. "Are you taking meds to stop yourself from shifting?"

I can't imagine purposefully repressing my bear.

"N-No." Ishmael pressed closer to Madagascar and away from Payson. "I-I mean, yeah. I t-take meds, but I-I'm not a sh-shifter." His cheeks darkened further, and a fresh wave of embarrassment perfumed the air. "Th-They're for something else."

"Back off, Payson," Kontra ordered, his dark eyes narrowing. "You're freaking out Madagascar's mate."

At least it got him talking again, though . . . and leaning into me for support.

Payson obeyed by plopping on his ass and resting his forearms on his upturned knees. "So, whatcha takin' them for, big guy?"

Ishmael's focus moved to the floor in front of him, and he nibbled his bottom lip. Furrowing his brows, he shook his head.

"You don't have to tell right now, Ishmael," Madagascar told his mate, his bear grumbling in discontent upon scenting Ishmael's skyrocketing unease. "We'll get to it another time." With a glance around, Madagascar added, "When there aren't so many around, okay?"

Glancing toward him before refocusing on the floor,

Ishmael simply nodded.

Payson opened his mouth, perhaps planning to press the issue, but a quick shake of the head from Kontra caused him to snap his mouth shut. Instead, he turned and focused on the bound captive. Arching a brow, Payson rose to his feet.

"You want me to take this one to Draven?" Payson asked, brushing off his butt as he headed toward him.

"Yes," Kontra confirmed, taking the sweat shorts that a recently arrived Tim handed to him. "We need to know what he knows."

The bound man cringed away from Payson, too, but probably for different reasons than Ishmael had. There was fear in the human's eyes, and he began shaking his head.

Madagascar knew that Draven was not only a warlock but a vampire. He would delve into the asshole's mind and give a report to Kontra. Then, depending on what he found, the man would either be put down for his crimes or his mind would be wiped, and he would be relocated.

As Payson tossed the man over his shoulder and headed out of the room, Ishmael whispered, "What are you gonna do to him?"

"That depends on his crimes," Kontra replied evasively. He turned to Lamar and asked, "Is everyone clear?"

"Vail's team is clear," Lamar told him. "And Adam's is exiting now."

"Good." Kontra patted Lamar on the shoulder and ordered, "Upload the virus. It's time to get out of here." As Lamar inserted a flash drive into a slot, Kontra turned to Ishmael. "Time to go, son. We have a lot to explain."

Madagascar rose, pleased when Ishmael didn't fight him when he urged him to stand.

"C-Can I get some stuff from my r-room?"

Upon hearing Ishmael's stuttered request, Madagascar gaped. "You live here?"

While Ishmael nodded while twisting his fingers together in obvious unease, he mumbled, "Yeah. So I can be monitored for safety."

Madagascar bit back a growl, wishing he could track down any of the assholes who'd filled Ishmael with whatever nonsense he clearly believed.

CHAPTER FOUR

Clutching his duffle bag to his chest, Ishmael struggled to keep his breathing even. He couldn't see much through the tint of the windows, but he figured there wasn't really much to see, since it was dark outside. Ishmael wished the sun had been shining so he could watch where they were going.

I bet the views would be lovely. I haven't been outside farther than the picnic area at the facility in . . . I don't know how long.

Ishmael didn't drive, and most of the staff just ignored him. A couple of the guards had offered to drive him places, but he hadn't liked the way they looked at him when they didn't think he would notice, so he'd always declined. Plus, sometimes, when they didn't realize it, he'd overheard them talking about him. They would call him names even as they made bets about who would pop his cherry.

While Ishmael wasn't totally certain what that meant, he didn't think it was a good thing, considering how they spoke about it.

Where am I going now?

Ishmael hadn't seen anyone else from the facility being taken in the SUV. Instead, he was sitting next to Madagascar and surrounded by the handsome man's buddies. They claimed they weren't bad guys, but Ishmael had seen them removing the animals from their cages and loading them into a couple of big box trucks.

Where are they taking them?

If I asked, would they tell me the truth?

If I somehow got away, where would I go?

Without his phone, Ishmael couldn't call Doctor Meyer. He didn't have her phone number memorized. He'd never gone anywhere without it, so he hadn't even tried. The guy who'd taken it hadn't given it back, and he didn't think he would even if Ishmael asked him.

They think they're the good guys. Why do they think that?

Ishmael opened his mouth, thinking about asking, but he snapped his mouth shut again just as quickly.

Madagascar reached over and gently unpeeled one hand from his grip on his bag. With a warm smile, he threaded their fingers together. Then Madagascar squeezed that hand lightly.

"If you have something to say, you're allowed to say it, Ishmael," Madagascar told him softly. "I don't want you to think you're a prisoner." His expression took on an uncomfortable twist as he murmured, "Even though you may feel like that right now."

"I-I'm your p-prisoner?" Ishmael mumbled. He'd figured as much, but saying it out loud made it so much scarier. "Why?" Hunching his shoulders, Ishmael whispered, "What do you want with me?"

"To make you happy."

Ishmael gaped upon hearing Madagascar's softly spoken statement.

Madagascar lifted his free hand and gently touched Ishmael's jaw, sending a fissure of tingles cascading down his neck. "I know you don't believe me right now, Ish," he rumbled softly. "I hope in time that you will." Furrowing his black brows, Madagascar told him, "And in the meantime, I'll do what I can to make your time with us as painless and pleasurable as possible."

"P-Pleasurable?" Ishmael whispered, feeling a shiver travel down his spine. "What, uh—" He swallowed hard as his belly flipped oddly. "What do you mean?"

Madagascar growled for an instant before he cut it off with a cough. After rubbing a palm over his goateed face, he smiled wryly at Ishmael. "Sorry, Ish," he murmured. "Thinking of you and pleasure at the same time makes me think of all the sweat-inducing things I'd like to do with you . . . to you."

Understanding dawned on Ishmael, and he felt his cheeks heat. "Y-You're talking about, uh—" He glanced around the vehicle, but no one seemed to be paying them any attention where they were sitting on the rear bench seat. Still, Ishmael lowered his voice when he stated, "Sex."

Nodding once, Madagascar told him, "Yes, Ishmael." He began using his thumb to lightly massage Ishmael's knuckles. "I'm talking about sex. Your sexy body, your scent, your kind heart, they all turn me on very much."

Ishmael felt the butterflies bumping in his belly begin to move lower, and his prick began to thicken behind his fly. Shifting in his seat, he mumbled, "I like your cologne, too." Having never done anything with anyone before, he nibbled his bottom lip as he struggled with what else to say. "Um, a-and you're very h-handsome."

"Thank you, Ishmael," Madagascar rumbled. "And I'm not wearing cologne. Shifters normally don't because of our enhanced sense of smell."

Sighing, Ishmael frowned. "Why does everyone keep talking about shifters?" He shook his head even as he stated firmly, "Doctor Meyer explained it to me. There's no such thing." After a second of hesitation, Ishmael added, "I used to have delusions brought on from the smoke and chemicals I accidentally inhaled in the fire. Thoughts of turning into a wolf, but Doctor Meyer figured it out, and with my medication, I don't have them anymore." Seeing the way Madagascar's brows shot up, Ishmael hurried to say, "Maybe if that guy gives me back my phone, I can call the doctor, and we can go see her. I bet she could help you, too."

For an instant, Madagascar appeared shocked. His brown eyes were wide, and he opened and closed his mouth. Then he seemed to shake himself out of it, and he lifted his free hand and again traced along Ishmael's jaw with the backs of his fingers.

"Thank you for sharing that with me," Madagascar rumbled with a smile. "That's important information for us to have." Then his smile faded, and he shook his head. "I don't know how you really ended up with those people, but I hope we can find out."

"I told you," Ishmael insisted. "There was a fire. I—"

"I know you believe that, Ishmael," Madagascar cut in, which Ishmael thought was a little rude. "I figure that's what they've been telling you, but I don't actually think it's true."

Frowning, Ishmael muttered, "You shouldn't interrupt people. It's rude."

"My apologies, Ishmael," Madagascar quickly told him. "I'll try to be more mindful of that in the future."

Ishmael nodded, mollified. "Okay." Then he found himself asking, "Why do you think it's not true?" Scowling at the handsome black man, Ishmael wondered, "What would be the point of lying? Doctor Meyer made sure I had a comfortable room there and a job. She's nice."

Maybe a little stern on occasion, but nice.

"I really don't have an answer to all those questions, Ishmael," Madagascar told him, obviously being truthful. "I'm hoping the guys can help us find out, though."

Before Madagascar could say more, he felt the vehicle slow. He leaned toward the window, looking out. A clearing opened before him, and he could make out a nice house with a turret thingy on the left side and a wrap-around porch. Lights flooded from the windows, illuminating a garage off to one side.

Perhaps due to the rumble of the vehicles — the motorcycles some of the guys were driving were awfully loud, after all —

a number of figures were pouring from the house.

"Oh," Ishmael whispered, surprised to see a couple of animals easing from the forest and a wolf trotting out of the house. Uncertainty flooded him as Sam parked the SUV. Ishmael glanced toward Madagascar, who was watching him with a concerned look on his face, before looking back toward the yard. Ishmael wasn't certain he wanted to get out of the vehicle.

"No one will hurt you, Ishmael," Madagascar told him quietly. "The doc will need to draw blood and check your vitals, but he's going to be doing that to all the shifters we rescued."

Even as Ishmael nodded, he muttered, "But I'm not a shifter." Doctor Meyer had explained it to him many times.

Madagascar sighed softly but didn't refute him. Instead, he leaned forward and followed the other guys out of the vehicle. With their hands still joined, Madagascar urged Ishmael to follow.

After a few seconds of hesitation, Ishmael did so. He stopped outside the open door, his bag in one hand, holding Madagascar's tightly with the other. He swallowed hard as he watched all the activity, shock filling him when many of the men were greeted by other men with hugs and deep kisses.

"A-Are they . . . couples?" Ishmael murmured.

"Yes, Ish," Madagascar confirmed. "Many of these guys are shifters and have mates of their own."

Huh. Bad guys have someone love them?

Ishmael didn't know how that worked. If they weren't good people and did bad things, why would someone love them? Then again, he'd heard the expression love is blind, so maybe that was it.

Or maybe they're not really bad after all . . . or not that bad.

Madagascar squeezed Ishmael's hand to get his attention. "And I hope that once you understand what was really going on at that facility, you'll accept what I'm telling you." The large black male hesitated an instant, his smile appearing a little tentative. "And you'll accept that I'm your mate." With another squeeze to Ishmael's hand, Madagascar told him, "It's one of the reasons we feel so naturally drawn to each other. We're connected right down to our souls."

Standing next to each other, Ishmael realized he actually stood an inch taller than Madagascar. He hadn't really noticed while at the facility due to how crazy everything seemed . . . and the pain from his arm. The pain pill that Ryan had given him had worked really well, though, because Ishmael barely felt it anymore. Ishmael had thought Madagascar was bigger than him, but that wasn't actually the case.

Maybe it just seems that way because of his strong, assured personality.

"I-I don't really know what that means," Ishmael admitted softly. "Are souls a real thing?"

"Oh, yes," Madagascar assured, his smile growing larger. "They are." Then movement off to the side caught the other man's attention. "And now you get to meet my family."

Ishmael looked where Madagascar was and took an involuntary step backward, but his back hit the side of the SUV. There was nowhere to go. He felt a tremble work through him as he watched the approach of five large black men, one big white guy, and a little white guy.

"Y-Your family?" Ishmael whispered.

Boy, do they look intimidating. What if they don't like me?

Even as the thought popped into Ishmael's head, he wondered why he cared. Maybe it was because Madagascar was talking about soul mates. That was a term for partner, right?

Ishmael was becoming more confused by the second.

"Easy, Ishmael." Madagascar rested his free hand on Ishmael's chest and rubbed over his pectoral. "They're good guys. You'll like them."

Before Ishmael could tell Madagascar that that wasn't his concern, he spotted Kontra roll up the back door of the box truck. "Okay, guys," the big man stated, taking a step back.

"If you can get down on your own, feel free. For those of you too injured to make the step, we'll help. Just give us a minute." Kontra actually smiled warmly as he took a step back. "I know the trees look inviting, and you'd probably love to go for a run, but try to restrain yourself. I know it sucks," he continued as if the animals inside could actually understand his words. "But we do need to take blood samples and check your vitals. That way, we can figure out what shit those scientists have been pumping into your system and help your body heal from it."

Then a large bobcat carefully hopped from the back, followed by a tiger and a fox.

Gaping, Ishmael shook his head. "He doesn't have any leashes or anything." Fear rushed through his veins for a new reason. "W-What if they attack him?" Ishmael snapped his attention to Madagascar. "Or us?"

Madagascar smiled even as he sighed. "Ishmael, they won't attack him or us," he told him, rubbing his chest again. "Those are shifters. They understand every word Kontra said."

Ishmael returned his attention to Kontra and the animals, surprised to find them all lying around docilely as a very tall, very slender man approached with a bag in hand.

"Wha?" Even as Ishmael watched the animals allow the men to touch, poke, and prod, disbelief at what he watched filled him. "H-How?"

Feeling completely overwhelmed, Ishmael couldn't stop it when he felt his eyes roll to the back of his head, darkness taking him, and he dropped.

CHAPTER FIVE

"Ish!"

Madagascar barely managed to get his arms around Ishmael in time to keep the huge male from dropping to the ground and possibly hitting his head. Even with his shifter strength, he didn't think he could swing his mate into his arms and carry him. Ishmael was just too large.

Easing to his knees, Madagascar positioned Ishmael beside him. He rested his mate's head against his chest. Madagascar held Ishmael tightly with one arm while threading his fingers through the other shifter's hair with the other.

"Mads," Congo called, picking up a jog toward him. "What happened?" His brother squatted next to him. "Who's this?" Picking up Ishmael's wrist, Congo appeared to be checking his pulse. "His pulse is steady and strong."

Madagascar met Congo's concerned expression with a smile. "This is Ishmael Cartwright," he told his brother, pride filling his tone. "And he's my mate."

Congo's eyes widened, and Madagascar noticed similarly shocked looks on the faces of the others. His cousin Valentine snapped out of it first. The other brown bear shifter grinned broadly.

"Hell, yeah, Mads!" Valentine clenched a fist and thrust it in the air in a show of triumph. "Congratulations!"

The others exchanged looks. Then, as one, the five brown bears tipped their heads back and roared, expressing their happiness for him. Zhaul laughed, grinning, while Evan smiled shyly from where he was tucked close to Shannon's side.

When the noise quieted—Madagascar was a little surprised that their roars hadn't woken Ishmael—he grinned up at the group. "Thanks, guys." With a scoffing laugh, he admitted, "Sure didn't expect that to happen when I went on this assignment."

"I'm signing up for the next one," Valentine declared, lifting his hand in the air as if volunteering for something.

Zion laughed as he patted Eurik on the stomach, exchanging a look with the other shifter. "We all will, right?"

Eurik nodded. "Totally." Reaching forward, he patted Madagascar on the shoulder. "Lucky bastard."

Madagascar nodded. "I really am."

Resting on one knee before him, Congo eyed Ishmael. "What happened to him?" he asked, worry replacing his elation. "Should I get Eli? He's dressed as opposed to the others being in animal form."

"Well, there's a bit of a story there," Madagascar admitted. Then he took a few minutes to explain everything that had happened and what he'd learned about Ishmael.

"Damn," Evan mumbled, his cheeks taking on a pinkish hue. "Another brainwashed mate. Between the witches and scientists, I don't know who's worse."

"A definite draw," Shannon agreed, dipping his head to press a kiss to Evan's temple. "Want help getting him into the house?" Eyeing Ishmael's bulging muscles, he mused, "I wonder if that's how he looked before they did whatever to him."

Congo shook his head slowly, his black brows furrowing. "What really concerns me is . . . why did they keep him alive in human form to work as a janitor?"

Madagascar shrugged. "I'm just grateful they did."

"True that," Valentine stated sagely. Then he moved to Ishmael's other side and slipped an arm around him, being mindful of his injured arm. "Room in the house or one of our tents?"

"Is there an empty room?" Madagascar asked curiously while he and Valentine lifted his mate. He would definitely favor having a bed for his mate while claiming him.

Once he's ready. And gods, I hope it won't be too long.

"Yeah," Congo assured, rising, too. He peered toward the group of newly freed shifters. "I'll let Kontra know we're taking him to the second bedroom on the right upstairs, and that we'll need Eli, Sam, or Ryan before too long." As Madagascar nodded and they started moving, Congo added, "Maybe if he sees all of us camping out back, humans and animals coexisting, he'll come around quicker."

After uttering those hopeful words, Congo began striding swiftly toward where Kontra worked with a number of others on the rescued shifters.

Between the four of them—Shannon and Eurik each grabbed a leg, too—they carried Ishmael to the indicated room. Evan and Zhaul hurried before them. The pair quickly pulled down the comforter and sheet and arranged the pillows.

Once Madagascar had Ishmael settled on the bed, he moved to the foot of it. His mate's feet nearly hung off the end, and he carefully removed his mate's boots and socks, setting them aside. Madagascar hesitated, wondering if it would be too intrusive to remove his shirt or pants. Deciding it would, he grabbed the sheet and pulled it up over him.

With a sigh, Madagascar stared at his sleeping mate, unable to get enough of the sight of the man. He desperately wanted to strip him and trace every inch of his big body. Madagascar's fingers twitched with his desires.

"I'm happy for you, man." Valentine slung his arm around Madagascar's shoulders, a grin on his lips. "Even if it takes a little work, you know it'll be worth it." Then he winked before releasing him. "Be patient. I'm sure it won't take long for him

33

to come around. You know how Fate works."

Madagascar nodded. "From your lips to Fate's ears."

"Hey, Mads," Ryan greeted, walking into the room followed by Congo. He carried a satchel over his shoulder. "Figured I'd take advantage of Ishmael being unconscious and take his blood." Setting the bag on top of the dresser, Ryan swept his gaze over Ishmael while opening it. "I imagine he fainted from getting overwhelmed, but we'll keep an eye on him, just in case."

Easing onto the edge of the bed, Madagascar couldn't resist taking Ishmael's hand again. "Thanks, Ryan."

"Okay." Ryan approached with a few supplies. "Let's get this done so we can send it to Lark in Stone Ridge to be tested."

Ryan quickly and efficiently took three vials of blood. After wrapping them and placing them in the bag, he returned to the bed's side. He checked Ishmael's pulse as well as the wound on his arm.

"I don't see any signs of infection," Ryan declared, rewrapping Ishmael's arm. "For now, I'm thinking rest, food, and fluids." With a pat to Madagascar's shoulder, Ryan told him, "I'll leave a pain pill with you for him."

After tucking everything away, Ryan pulled out a small pill bottle. He shook one pale yellow tablet onto the dresser. Ryan closed the lid and tucked the bottle into the bag.

"How long do you think he'll sleep?" Madagascar wondered, hoping Ryan had some idea.

Shaking his head, Ryan shrugged. "Tough to say. He could have already been tired from working at the facility, or he could be really stressed out from everything that's happened this evening." He pointed at Ishmael's arm. "I know he's a shifter, but his system is probably compromised by whatever shit was in the pills they convinced him to take."

"Okay. Thanks, Ryan." Madagascar watched as Ryan

saluted, picked up the satchel, and headed out of the room. He sighed and relaxed against the headboard. Peering around at the members of his bear sleuth, Madagascar smiled, feeling fatigue begin to fill him as the adrenaline from the incursion into the facility began to drain from him. "Thanks for your help, guys."

"You're welcome, bro," Congo replied with a smile. Pointing between them, he encouraged, "You should climb into bed with him." Congo held up his hand, palm out, to stall Madagascar's comment about how presumptuous that was, and told him, "I know what you're thinking, but you're both shifters. The skin-on-skin contact will kickstart the need to cement your bond, even in him."

Letting out a chuckle mixed with a groan, Madagascar admitted, "I don't know if I'll be able to control myself."

"You will, Mads," Congo replied confidently. "I have faith in you." After patting his leg, he turned toward the door. "There's still a few hours of night left. Take advantage of it." Congo ushered the others out the door — the men offering another round of congratulations as they went — and told him, "We'll plan to bring you breakfast an hour or so after daylight, but if you need something sooner, just holler."

"Thanks again, guys."

After Congo closed the door behind him, Madagascar leaned over and untied his boots. He toed them off, removing his socks next. Standing, Madagascar stripped off his shirt before hesitating with his fingers over his fly.

Considering Madagascar didn't wear underwear, he decided just unbuttoning his jeans would have to do. He pulled back the sheet and stared at his sleeping mate. Since Ishmael's long-sleeved shirt was already ruined — Ryan had cut off one sleeve to get at his wound — Madagascar decided to grow a claw and remove it in pieces.

Madagascar eased into the bed next to Ishmael and pulled

up the sheet. After a few seconds of hesitation, he slid his arm under his mate's body. Unable to resist, Madagascar rolled the bigger man toward him, placing Ishmael's injured arm across his chest and his head on his shoulder.

The skin-on-skin contact caused the hairs on his arms to stand on end, and he let out a deep sigh of contentment. He stared up at the ceiling for a few moments, listening to Ishmael breathe. Madagascar felt his mate's warm breath ghosting across his chest, and his nipples beaded.

Doing his best to ignore the way his cock throbbed behind the fly of his jeans, Madagascar closed his eyes. He enjoyed his mate's delicious aroma and matched his breathing to the other man. When Ishmael snuffled a little in his sleep and nuzzled his cheek against Madagascar's chest, he couldn't help but smile.

Reveling in the simple pleasure of holding Ishmael in his arms, Madagascar slowly drifted off to sleep.

Chapter Six

Rousing slowly, Ishmael relaxed with his eyes closed. He couldn't remember the last time he'd slept so deeply and so soundly. Maybe it was because the bed felt so wonderfully comfortable, and there was a scent surrounding him that he wanted to wallow in.

Ishmael also couldn't remember when he'd woken with such an aching morning wood. Normally, he would need to coax his half-mast prick to life if he decided to whack off. Right then, Ishmael felt as if he could roll to his stomach, grind against the mattress, immerse himself in that wonderful smell, and get off in less than a minute.

Except. Why? My bed at the facility doesn't feel like this.

With that thought, Ishmael grew a bit more aware . . . and he realized he wasn't alone in the bed. He snapped his eyes open in surprise. The dark-skinned chest under his cheek registered. Lifting his gaze along the broad torso, Ishmael took in the miles of thick muscles, and he felt his dick twitch.

Oh wow boy howdy!

Finally, Ishmael's attention reached the man's face, and he felt his breath catch in his throat. He recognized Madagascar's goateed features, his face relaxed in sleep. Ishmael felt the urge to lift his hand and trace his fingertips along the thin line of hair framing his full lips.

He's holding me in his arms. Sleeping with me. What would his lips feel like?

As Ishmael stared and wondered, Madagascar's eyelids slid up.

Ishmael froze, wondering what Madagascar would think of how they had been sleeping. Would he be upset to be in bed with him, holding him? Except, he didn't even know how he'd ended up in bed with the man.

"Good morning, handsome," Madagascar rumbled, his voice deep and rough from sleep. Lifting a hand, he threaded it through Ishmael's shaggy hair, pushing it away from his face. "Did you sleep okay?"

"Yeah," Ishmael whispered. Suddenly feeling shy, he lowered his gaze to the man's chin. "Um, h-how'd I get here?"

Sliding his hand down along Ishmael's face, Madagascar teased his fingers under his chin. He applied a bit of pressure, encouraging him to lift his gaze. Once Ishmael met Madagascar's gaze again, Madagascar smiled warmly at him.

"You got a little overwhelmed when we first arrived last night," Madagascar told him. Then his brows furrowed, and he smirked. "Well, this morning, really."

"I did?" Ishmael searched his memory for the last thing he remembered. The scene of Kontra and his people handling docile animals from the facility popped into his head. "Oh." Ishmael gaped. "Y-Your people, uh, the animals." After clearing his throat, he muttered, "They almost seemed . . . friendly."

Madagascar smiled encouragingly. "Yes. Maybe not friendly, per se," he mused quietly. "They were definitely happy to be removed from the cages and were probably grateful for Kontra's people's help." Scoffing softly, Madagascar told him, "I know when I first realized the warlocks in Kontra's gang weren't going to use their magick against us and force us to do cruel things, I was damn grateful to them."

Ishmael frowned. "Warlocks? Magick?" Sometimes, Madagascar made such outlandish comments, and he didn't know how to process them. They went against everything he'd been taught by Doctor Meyer. With a sigh, Ishmael muttered, "I don't understand why you believe in that stuff."

Clicking his tongue, Madagascar shrugged the shoulder not under Ishmael's cheek. "Maybe after we've both had our morning coffee, we'll discuss this more." His eyes narrowed, and a smile that looked . . . hungry . . . creased his lips. "Right now, there's definitely something else I'm interested in discussing . . . and doing."

While Madagascar had been speaking, he'd begun to slide his palm down Ishmael's side. The glide of the man's calloused hand over his skin created a wash of tingles to spread across his flesh. His gut clenched as warmth flooded it, flowing swiftly down to his groin.

Gasping in surprise, Ishmael shifted a bit on the bed. He felt his erection rub against Madagascar's hip. Even through the fabric of his jeans, the pressure felt fantastic.

"Mads," Ishmael moaned, a shudder working through him. "Oh. What are you . . ."

"I can stop, if you want, Ish," Madagascar told him, his eyes narrowing a little. "But I really don't want to." He moved his hand behind Ishmael's back and slipped his fingers beneath the waistband, teasing along the top of his butt cheek. "I want to help take care of that impressive rod digging into my hip." Ishmael would have felt embarrassed to have his arousal so blatantly pointed out, but then Madagascar's voice lowered to a husky rumble as he continued, "I want to please you, handsome. Would you let me suck your cock?"

"S-Suck on my, my d-dick?" Ishmael barely got the words out, and he barely held back his orgasm just from thinking of the handsome man's full lips offering to apply wet pressure to his sensitive shaft. "Y-You'd really, r-really do that?"

"Oh, yes, Ish," Madagascar rumbled gruffly. Sliding his hand out of his pants, moving it to his hip, he gripped him and pushed lightly. "Lie back, baby," Madagascar encouraged. "Let me make you feel good."

Letting out a whine of need, Ishmael did as he'd been told. He desperately wanted to feel that. He'd heard about it. He'd seen others in secluded corners giving each other blowjobs, but no one had offered to give him one.

Ishmael watched with anticipation as Madagascar rolled to his hands and knees. The lust blazing from his eyes made it hard for Ishmael to take a full breath. He panted swiftly as he watched Madagascar ease closer and reach for the fly of his jeans.

When Madagascar paused, Ishmael couldn't stop his groan of dismay.

"Relax, my mate," Madagascar purred, resting a hand on Ishmael's stomach. "I just want permission," he explained, rubbing over his abdominals lightly. "Need to hear you say you're okay with me sucking you."

"Yes," Ishmael blurted out swiftly. "Please, yes, please." When Madagascar began to grin, he ordered, "Suck me."

"With pleasure."

Madagascar growled even as he grinned. At the same time, he popped the button on Ishmael's fly. Then he lowered the zipper.

The release of pressure yanked a deep moan from Ishmael. The relief felt absolutely amazing, even while leaving him needing more. When Madagascar lifted the waistband of his underwear and began tugging it down, Ishmael quickly lifted his hips, and his cock popped free.

"Oh, Ish," Madagascar rumbled, his dark eyes seeming to blaze with some inner light. "You're absolutely stunning."

Madagascar skimmed the backs of his forefingers up the bottom of Ishmael's shaft in obvious appreciation, sending sparks down his erection to his balls. The sensations caused his gut to clench, and he felt the tell-tale tingle of need at the base of his spine. Gripping the sheets beneath him in a tight hold, Madagascar did his best to push it back. A bead of precum oozed from his slit.

"Mads," Ishmael whined, shifting restlessly on the sheet. "P-Please."

"Your wish, handsome," Madagascar murmured, leaning close. After blowing a breath across his damp crown, he finished, "My command."

Then, to Ishmael's absolute delight, Madagascar opened his mouth and wrapped his lips around his swollen knob. The heat hit him first, and he gasped sharply at the exquisite sensation. When Madagascar sucked, Ishmael arched and moaned.

Madagascar rested his hands on Ishmael's hips, easing him back to the bed. At the same time, he swallowed more of his shaft. The feel of Madagascar's tongue teasing at the sensitive bit of flesh beneath his crown nearly caused his eyes to roll back in his head.

"Mads!" Ishmael cried, a shudder rolling through his body. Feeling Madagascar ease partway off, sucking hard, then sink down on him again, Ishmael felt his balls tighten. Opening his mouth, he managed to squeak, "C-Clo—"

Then Ishmael's orgasm erupted through him. Fiery tingles flooded his veins, shaking him to the core. His thighs clenched and released in time with the pulses surging up his erection.

Floating on the bliss of his release, Ishmael panted raggedly, shivering and twitching. He barely felt it when Madagascar eased off his prick. The feel of the other man gliding his hands up his torso, pausing to tweak his nipples, extended his pleasure, drawing another moan from him.

"Oh, Ish," Madagascar rumbled, his voice thick and rough. "So fucking sexy, my mate."

Peeling open eyelids he hadn't even realized he'd closed, Ishmael peered up at Madagascar with a loopy-feeling smile. His eyes snapped wider when he noticed Madagascar's arm movement. Following it, he found himself staring at another man's hard erection for the first time in his life.

"Oh, wow," Ishmael whispered, feeling his fingers twitch. The man's big black dick was a thing of beauty—long and thick. His balls hung large and swollen below the base, and Ishmael longed to cradle the heavy orbs. Lifting a hand on instinct, Ishmael murmured, "Can I?"

Madagascar snapped his attention to Ishmael's gaze. His chest heaved as he released himself, as if it had been a huge effort. Easing forward, Madagascar straddled Ishmael's hips, causing his twitching dick to swing over Ishmael's abdominals.

"I'd love to feel your touch, Ish," Madagascar told him thickly. Resting his forearms on either side of Ishmael's head, he purred, "Nothing would please me more."

After a hard swallow, Ishmael gave in to his desire. He lifted his left hand and gently cradled Madagascar's balls. When the other man gasped, he jerked his attention back up to Madagascar's face. The heavy-lidded expression the man sported caused a fresh wash of arousal to surge through his body. Ishmael's prick even threatened to rise again, which he'd never experienced before.

Ishmael returned his attention to Madagascar's groin and wrapped his right hand around the man's thick shaft. He squeezed the man's prick as he began to slowly jack him. Hearing Madagascar groan his name, he felt a swell of power and pride filling him.

I did this to this strong man.

"Faster, mate," Madagascar urged roughly. "Please, faster."

Doing as Madagascar bid, Ishmael obeyed. He sped up his hand jacking the man's prick, tightening it a little for good measure. At the same time, he gently rolled Madagascar's balls just the way he liked.

"Yesssss," Madagascar hissed through clenched teeth. He

panted harshly, his nostrils flaring. His chest heaved, and a shudder worked through him. "Ish."

Ishmael felt Madagascar's balls draw up. An instant later, the erection in his hold jerked and swelled before a thick burst of cum erupted from the head. The jet of white cream splattered over Ishmael's chest, warming his skin. Pride flooding him, Ishmael continued to work Madagascar, causing more and more sprays of seed to mark his chest. Ishmael didn't know why, but having Madagascar's white cream covering him turned him on a lot, and his prick began to swell once more.

"My mate," Madagascar rumbled thickly. His satiated smile curved his lips as he peered down at Ishmael. "Your touch is magick." Then his attention flicked to Ishmael's renewed arousal, and he grinned at him. "Looks like you enjoyed that as much as me."

Feeling a blush rise up his cheeks, Ishmael peered over Madagascar's shoulder, uncertain what to say.

"I didn't mean to embarrass you, handsome," Madagascar told him, sliding his hand up to cup his jaw. "I think it's sexy."

"You do?" Ishmael snapped his attention back to Madagascar's face, wondering if that was true.

Madagascar nodded. "Very much so."

Dipping his head, Madagascar pressed his lips to Ishmael's lightly.

Ishmael moaned softly, lifting his hands to Madagascar's upper arms. He parted his lips, wanting more of his very first kiss. Madagascar didn't disappoint, and he dipped his tongue into Ishmael's mouth.

For an instant, Ishmael found himself surprised to find his own flavor on Madagascar's tongue. He moaned into the other man's mouth as he thought about his new lover swallowing his seed. Just as Madagascar had marked Ishmael on the outside, Ishmael had marked his lover on the inside.

Something deep within him, something primal, roared with pleasure at that knowledge.

Mine!

Ishmael didn't know or understand where that voice in his head came from, but he found himself agreeing with it.

A second later, Ishmael felt something weird going on with his teeth. He turned his head, breaking the kiss. His attention fell on Madagascar's neck.

Unable to help himself, as if someone else had control of him, Ishmael struck. He sank his strangely long teeth into the flesh where Madagascar's neck met his shoulder. The sweet nectar that flowed into his mouth yanked a deep, satisfied groan from him as he swallowed it.

When Ishmael sucked a second mouthful down his throat, his gut clenched. His balls pulled tight, and a fresh orgasm rocked through him. Arching, releasing Madagascar's neck, Ishmael roared his pleasure.

It wasn't until Ishmael began to come down from his endorphin high that he realized what he'd done.

Jerking his gaze to Madagascar's neck, Ishmael spotted the blood dribbling from his lover's neck. Unable to believe — or understand — his behavior, he cringed and turned his head, fearing a blow or sneer.

"I'm sorry," Ishmael whined, fearing Madagascar would think he was a freak. "I'm so sorry."

When was the last time I took my meds? I was supposed to take one after work last night. But, oh god, I didn't! I must be having a delusion.

CHAPTER SEVEN

Coming down from one of the most intense orgasms of his life, Madagascar panted heavily. He felt a slight tingle at his neck, and he lifted a shaky hand to it. When his fingers came away sticky, Madagascar stared in shock at the blood on his fingers.

Holy fucking shit. My mate just claimed me.

Finally, Ishmael's words registered to Madagascar's blissed-out brain. He snapped his attention to Ishmael, and his gut tightened, and not with pleasure.

His poor confused mate had his arms wrapped around his torso. He had his chin tipped down and his face turned to the side, as if he were trying to hide. His gorgeous mate apologized over and over, looking for all the world as if he were about to be punished in some way.

Maybe someone used to punish him?

Dismissing the thought for later, Madagascar eased to the left, propping himself up on his arm. He kept his leg slung over his mate's thighs, hoping the contact would help. Gently, he gripped Ishmael's wrist and squeezed lightly. When that didn't get a response, Madagascar slid his hand up and cradled Ishmael's jaw.

"Hey, Ish," Madagascar purred, rubbing his thumb along his jaw. "Look at me, handsome. Everything is okay."

It took Madagascar repeating his words twice more before Ishmael began to calm down. His mate peered at him from beneath his lashes. Nibbling his bottom lip, Ishmael appeared so conflicted and confused.

"There you are, Ishmael," Madagascar murmured, smiling at him. "You didn't do anything wrong. It's okay."

Ishmael's brows furrowed. His focus flicked to Madagascar's neck before returning to his face. He did that twice before he licked his lips.

"But," Ishmael whispered. "I-I bit you." He even lifted a hand and pointed. "Right there."

"I know you did," Madagascar responded, sliding his hand up to tease his fingers into Ishmael's thick black hair. "I liked it." When he saw the clear disbelief in Ishmael's dark eyes, Madagascar told him, "Your bite made me orgasm." Unable to keep it to himself, he added, "And when I eventually bite you, I know you will, too."

Frowning, Ishmael remained quiet for several heartbeats. He opened his mouth, then closed it again.

Madagascar waited patiently, wondering what Ishmael would say.

Finally, Ishmael simply asked, "Why?"

Not understanding the context, Madagascar hesitated. "Uh." He cocked his head as he gave Ishmael a rueful smile. "I'm not certain which part you're asking about. Why what?"

"Why did I bite you?" Ishmael asked. Before Madagascar could answer, his mate continued with, "I've never done anything with anyone before. Is biting normal when you have sex with someone? Is what we did considered sex?" Madagascar thought about what to answer first, even as his bear roared possessively in his mind upon learning that they would be the only person to ever touch their mate, but Ishmael wasn't done. "Did you really orgasm? Is that why you want me to bite you again? Why would you bite me? Will I orgasm?"

Smiling widely, Madagascar slipped his fingers to Ishmael's lips, quieting him. "Let's see if I can cover all those things," he murmured, thinking quickly. "Uh, yes, you'll orgasm," he told him, deciding to go backward. "And I'd bite you for two reasons. To give you pleasure and to complete our bond." Madagascar felt Ishmael open his mouth between his fingers, so he hurriedly continued, "Yes, I really did orgasm, and not only would I love to feel that again, your teeth in my neck also pleases me because it means you and your animal are claiming me back." With a growl, Madagascar admitted, "The fact that you don't ever remember doing anything with another makes me so hot, my mate." He couldn't help his feral smile as he added, "I can't wait to explore all of your interests, likes, and even your dislikes together."

Finally, Madagascar moved his hand back to Ishmael's jaw and waited.

Ishmael furrowed his brows. He inhaled deeply before licking his lips. He slipped his attention toward the ceiling as a myriad of emotions flitted across his face. Finally, his jaw clenched once before he frowned at Madagascar.

Uh oh.

Madagascar just knew he wasn't going to like what was coming.

"You keep saying that I have an animal, but that's just not true," Ishmael claimed, once again denying his heritage. "I'd know if I turned into an animal. And I don't."

Blowing out a breath, Madagascar jumped in with both feet and revealed, "That's because those pills you're taking are repressing your ability."

"Repressing?" Ishmael repeated the word slowly, as if struggling with it.

Madagascar didn't make him ask. "The pills stop your ability. They make it so you can't feel your animal." After a second of hesitation, he pressed, "Your wolf. Those memories of you changing into a wolf, they're not delusions, Ishmael. They really happened." When Ishmael continued to frown and even began to shake his head, Madagascar claimed, "That's why your teeth lengthened, and you bit me." He could feel the blood oozing from the wound, since Ishmael hadn't closed it, and he pointed at his flesh. "That's why you liked drinking my blood. Somewhere deep inside you, your wolf recognized that I'm your mate, and he claimed me."

By the time Madagascar finished speaking, Ishmael was practically vibrating with the way he shook his head. His lips were moving, but even Madagascar's heightened hearing didn't allow him to make out what he was saying. Finally, when he urged Ishmael to stop shaking his head so hard, his heart practically broke when he managed to read his lips.

Ishmael was repeating *no, no, no* over and over again.

Madagascar bit back a sigh, guilt flooding him as he realized he'd pushed too hard. Pressing close, he wrapped his arms around Ishmael and cradled him to his chest. He massaged the back of his neck with one hand while rubbing up and down his back with his other.

"I'm sorry, Ish," Madagascar murmured into his ear. "I didn't mean to upset you." He bussed a kiss to his mate's temple. "I just wanted to be honest."

"I want Doctor Meyer," Ishmael whined, pushing against Madagascar's chest. "She'll make it all better."

Grimacing, Madagascar sighed deeply. "I'm sorry, baby." He held tightly to Ishmael, hating that his mate was trying to get away from him. "I wish I could give you what you want, but she won't help. She's lying, and she'll only make it worse."

"No, she doesn't lie," Ishmael bellowed, surprising Madagascar with the intensity of his anger. "She helps me."

Realizing he was losing control of the situation damn fast, Madagascar figured he only had one option left. "I can prove it to you," he declared. "I can prove that shifters are real."

Ishmael snapped his mouth shut and froze. He stared at Madagascar for a long moment as if gauging his truthfulness. Ishmael even narrowed his eyes as if that would help him figure it out.

"How can you do that?" Ishmael asked, sounding wary. Then he snickered and asked, "The full moon ain't for another couple of weeks."

Scoffing, Madagascar appreciated the levity. "A shifter doesn't need a full moon to change," he claimed, rubbing along Ishmael's neck, wishing he'd had the wherewithal to bite his mate back. Madagascar longed for the day when he would see his mark upon Ishmael's neck. "Shifters can change anytime they want."

"Then how come they didn't change in their cage and ask to get out?" Ishmael frowned as he added, "I think I remember you saying that those animals were shifters and that they understood Kontra when he spoke to them." Pinning a narrow-eyed gaze upon Madagascar, as if he'd made some great point, Ishmael added, "So why didn't they prove they're not an animal and get released?"

Madagascar sighed, hating that he had to destroy Ishmael's illusion about the woman he obviously trusted and looked up to. "The facility didn't want to experiment on regular animals," he told him softly, earnestly. "They knew they were working on shifters. And they don't care that shifters are sentient. They want to exploit our gifts."

"Gifts?" Ishmael again looked confused. "What gifts?"

Madagascar hesitated, then began explaining shifter one-oh-one. He shared about their increased speed and strength, their heightened senses, and their vitality. He even admitted that a shifter lived upward of five hundred years, and that was why he could be over one hundred years and still look like he was in his thirties.

Shaking his head slowly, Ishmael muttered, "I think you're gonna have to prove it."

Nodding, accepting that, Madagascar murmured, "Like they say, a picture is worth a thousand words." He leaned down and pecked a kiss to Ishmael's lips, pleased when he didn't pull away. Staring into his mate's eyes, Madagascar asked, "Can you do me a favor first, though?"

Ishmael hesitated a second before nodding once. "Maybe."

Madagascar chuckled softly at that. "I know you enjoyed the taste of my blood," he revealed, indicating his neck. "Will you lick this clean, please?" When he saw Ishmael lean forward, then hesitate, he said, "Your saliva will help it scab over."

While that was a bit of a stretch, Madagascar figured Ishmael wouldn't be able to differentiate the scents between the truth and not. After all, Doctor Meyer had been lying to him for years. Finally, Ishmael nodded.

Holding his breath, Madagascar leaned closer to the man. Ishmael gripped his upper arms and pulled him down, and Madagascar was happy to go with it. When he felt the slide of Ishmael's wet tongue over his flesh, he couldn't hold in his soft moan.

"So good," Madagascar whispered, a tremble working through him. "Just damn."

Ishmael eased away from him, and he met his gaze with furrowed brows. "You really like that, huh?"

"Very much so," Madagascar confirmed with a quiet scoff. "Just . . . yeah. Just damn."

"Huh," Ishmael mumbled. Then his attention focused on Madagascar's neck, and his eyes widened. "Hey, it's already a scar. How'd that happen?"

Madagascar pecked a kiss to Ishmael's lips before explaining, "I told you a shifter has increased healing." Then he winked before adding, "And I'd been told that a mate's saliva has healing properties. Guess it's true." Hoping Ishmael would drop it, Madagascar began easing from the bed. "So, I'm going to shuck my clothes and shift into my bear. Don't worry," he assured, slipping from the bed. "Like I told you before. I understand everything and know my friends and family even when I'm in animal form."

"A-A b-bear?" Ishmael tensed, staring at him with wide eyes.

Thinking maybe a large brown bear wasn't the best to see right out of the gate, Madagascar asked, "Or would you like to see someone else shift? We have a couple of wolf shifters here that would be happy to shift for you." Grinning roguishly, Madagascar added, "Or something more exotic, like an elephant or camel? Something cute, like a penguin?"

"P-People believe they can change into those things?"

Madagascar didn't bother trying to correct the way Ishmael phrased the question. Instead, he nodded as he righted his jeans. "Yep." As he roved his gaze over Ishmael's still-open pants, he growled, "Of course, if you want to see one of them, you'll have to pull up your pants. We're not too concerned about nudity, as a rule, but I don't want anyone to see your sexy body unless you're shifting."

Ishmael didn't comment on that. Instead, he blushed as he eased from the bed and righted his underwear and pants. Then he grimaced as he began scratching at the now-dried semen Madagascar had left on his chest.

Damn, that's hot.

"There's a couple of bottles of water on the nightstand," Madagascar stated, heading toward them. "I'll soak your ruined shirt." As he cracked open a bottle and grabbed one of the shirt pieces from the floor, Madagascar admitted, "I cut it off you so you'd be more comfortable sleeping."

After soaking the fabric, Madagascar held it out to Ishmael. "Unless you'll let me clean you?"

Grabbing the cloth, Ishmael blushed once more. "Maybe later," he mumbled under his breath. He even went so far as to turn away as he began wiping himself down.

Madagascar decided he would have to wait until next time—when Ishmael was blissed out from pleasure—before he could enjoy the experience of cleaning up his lover.

Soon.

CHAPTER EIGHT

Eating breakfast outside was a novel experience for Ishmael. There were several cookfires in use—men cooking bacon, eggs, and sausages over them. On his way outside, Ishmael had passed the arch to the kitchen, and he'd spotted a couple of someones moving around in there, too.

When Ishmael had stepped out into the cool morning, he'd been shocked to see so many people milling around. Some were obviously still getting ready for the day, brushing their teeth with a tin cup in hand that Madagascar had explained was full of water. Most people wandered around only in a pair of shorts and either sandals or hiking boots.

Considering Ishmael still wasn't wearing a shirt, seeing that made him feel more comfortable.

"Come on, Ish," Madagascar urged, taking his hand and leading the way toward a couple of tents. "You didn't get to meet my family last night."

Ishmael felt a renewed feeling of trepidation, but he didn't really think he had a choice. Instead, he followed along behind his lover—*holy cow, I have a lover*. Peering at the big men through his lashes, Ishmael managed an uneasy smile as he was greeted by everyone. Not only did Madagascar give all the men's names, but also what animal they supposedly shifted into. The only small man was introduced as a warlock-in-training.

These guys sure seem certain about things.

Except, Ishmael realized if Madagascar was telling the truth, that meant Doctor Meyer had been lying to him for years. That thought caused bile to rise in his throat. As much as he didn't want all these nice, friendly men to really be the bad guys, Ishmael hated to think that the doctor had betrayed his trust even more.

"Ready for some coffee and food?" Madagascar asked as he slid an arm around his waist. "After our meal, I'll introduce you to a few others who would be happy to shift for you."

"I—"

Ishmael paused. Did he really want coffee if it wasn't expected of him? Everyone at the facility drank it, so when he'd started working there, it had always been included on his breakfast tray. Ishmael hadn't wanted to draw attention to himself, so he'd drink most of it before tossing the rest.

Madagascar did say he wanted to know more about me. Maybe —

"No one will give you shit that you want to see someone shift before accepting it, Ishmael," Madagascar told him, rubbing his back, clearly misunderstanding. "Just about every human has the exact same reaction as you."

"But you said I'm not human," Ishmael couldn't help pointing out.

Madagascar shrugged. "But you think you are." Leaning close, he pecked a kiss to Ishmael's lips, making him blush, and Madagascar grinned. "Come on." When they reached one of the fires, Madagascar pointed at the different carafes being kept warm on rocks. "What kind of coffee do you like? French roast, dark, decaf?"

There are different kinds of coffee?

Ishmael kept that thought to himself. While he figured it was possible that he would like one, he didn't want to risk it. Plus, if he didn't have to drink it to fit in, then he wanted to know that right up front.

Wait. Am I really thinking about staying?

If I'm with Madagascar and he's not lying about shifters, then yeah, I think I'd like that.

"I, uh—" Ishmael rubbed the back of his neck as he glanced

from the guy manning the coffee fire to Madagascar again. He leaned close to his lover and whispered, "I'm not a real big fan of coffee. Can I just have water, please?"

"Of course, buddy," the stranger replied, rising from where he'd been sitting. He held out his hand. "I'm Hunter, a human," he added with a smirk after Ishmael had taken his hand. After releasing him, Hunter told him, "And if you want something other than water, we have a couple of types of tea as well as several kinds of juice." Waving toward one of the carafes, he told him, "That's hot water. The tea bags are in the bag near it."

Ishmael hesitated before admitting, "I-I don't know if I like tea."

Hunter didn't bat an eyelash. He just nodded. "All right. Do you have a favorite kind of juice?" Using a thumb to point over his shoulder at the house, Hunter told him, "The ones I'm sure we have are orange juice, apple juice, and cranberry juice, but there could be others." He barked a laugh as he grinned broadly. "Hell, if you're a soda, lemonade, or energy drink in the morning guy, you'll probably find a few of those options in there, too."

"Uh, orange juice," Ishmael decided quickly, knowing he liked that. "Orange juice would be great."

"I'll get it for you." A small man sporting short, spikey black hair with white at the tips appeared next to Hunter. He grinned widely at him. "I'm Yuma." Holding out his hand, he added, "Penguin shifter, and this one's mate."

After Ishmael shook his hand, he murmured, "Penguin shifter." He looked at Madagascar. "Is he one of the ones you said wouldn't mind shifting for me?"

As Madagascar nodded, Yuma chuckled. "I'd be happy to shift for you." He grinned broadly as he stated, "Most humans think my penguin's cute, so it's easier for them the first time around." Yuma waved his hand absently. "A lot of these guys change into some pretty scary-looking animals. Lions and tigers and bears, oh my!" He ended with a snicker-snort.

"Really?" Ishmael peered at Madagascar. "Lions and tigers?"

Considering his lover claimed to be a brown bear and Zhaul had told him he was a giant panda, the bear part didn't surprise him.

"Yep." It was Hunter who responded. "That's Adam, and he's a white tiger." He pointed at a man with white-blond hair sitting at a nearby fire.

Obviously hearing his name, Adam looked in their direction and lifted a hand in a wave. "Hey, man."

Ishmael waved back tentatively.

"And that's Grimes, a lion shifter," Hunter continued, pointing at a large black-haired man. Ishmael knew who he meant because he followed up by saying, "The smaller guy on his lap is Chip. He's a bobcat shifter."

His mind reeling, Ishmael could only mutter, "Oh."

"Sorry to overwhelm ya, man," Hunter stated with an understanding smile. "Too many names and faces."

"I'll get your juice," Yuma once again proclaimed before trotting off toward the house.

"Time for breakfast," Madagascar stated after getting his own cup of coffee.

Feeling his stomach gurgle, Ishmael silently agreed.

"It's not real. It's not real." Ishmael stared at the penguin before him. Sitting on the ground from where he'd tripped and fallen, he wrapped his arms around his knees and rocked on his ass. "It's not real."

"Ishmael, it is real," Madagascar claimed, kneeling beside him. He had his arms wrapped around him, and even though the dark man continued talking, Ishmael couldn't resist pressing into him. "I told you what was going to happen, Ishmael.

Why do you think you're suddenly having a delusion now?"

Even though Madagascar sounded so calm and sure, Ishmael had to admit, "I haven't taken my medication in over thirty-six hours. I'm supposed to take it twice a day, and I missed last night and this morning."

A second later, icy cold water poured over Ishmael and Madagascar's heads. While Ishmael gasped and jolted, Madagascar snarled and jumped to his feet.

"What the hell, Payson?" Madagascar roared, clenching his hands into fists.

Payson shrugged, not looking at all perturbed by Madagascar's show of ire. "Ishmael doesn't believe that the penguin in front of him is real." He dropped the plastic cup onto the ground and crossed his arms over his chest. Smirking at Ishmael, Payson asked, "Do you believe I just poured cold water on your head?"

Ishmael winced as he felt his wet jeans mold uncomfortably to his legs. "Yeah," he muttered, brushing water from his eyes.

"Well, you can't have it both ways, man." Payson pointed at Yuma. "That's Yuma in penguin form, and I poured cold water on your head. Either both things happened, or neither of them happened." Reaching forward, Payson flipped a lock of soaked hair off Ishmael's forehead. "Which is it, man?"

Freezing, Ishmael realized he was suddenly faced with the truth. His shoulders slumped, and he whined softly. Once again, he wrapped his arms around his knees, and a second later, Madagascar was beside him, wrapping his arms around him, offering support.

Ishmael peered up at Madagascar as sadness filled him. "Doctor Meyer lied to me, didn't she?"

"I'm afraid so, baby," Madagascar confirmed, sadness filling his voice.

"Why?" Ishmael whined. "Why would someone do that?"

Payson sighed deeply as he crossed his legs and settled before them on the grass. "Look. I've been experimented on by scientists, too." He touched his nose. "It's why I ended up with such an awesome schnozz, but I lost the ability to recognize my mate." As if on cue, Land settled on Payson's lap, cuddling up to him, and Payson wrapped his human in a hug. "I had to fuck a lot of people and hope someday, my hyena would want them, too." Payson kissed the side of Land's neck, who stared at him adoringly even though he'd just mentioned fucking around . . . a lot. "Anyway, what I'm sayin' is, yeah, it sucks that these assholes are around doin' this shit to us, but don't let it stop you from movin' forward." After pecking a kiss to Land's lips, Payson grinned widely and waved around at the guys clustered around. "Ya got a helluva lot of guys here who'll help you get past it."

Ishmael nodded slowly, accepting the rather eccentric man's words. "Okay," he whispered. Then he frowned. "How do I do that? Move on, I mean?"

Yuma, back in human form, knelt beside them, already wearing a pair of shorts. "Reconnect with your wolf," he told him with a reassuring smile. "Focus on your hobbies. Enjoy time with your mate, family, and friends."

"And if you say you don't have any family, I'll smack you upside the back of your head, just like I would any of the guys," Congo stated with a soft growl and a frown. "You're my brother's mate. You're family."

Feeling a little warmth begin to ease the cold of having the truth revealed to him — or maybe that was the water — Ishmael smiled tentatively at Congo. The bear shifter was almost as intimidating as Kontra. He'd heard that bear was a grizzly, and he wasn't certain he wanted to see that shifter's animal anytime soon.

"And I'm a friend," Yuma piped up, raising his hand as he grinned broadly at him. "I've been traveling the world for decades, so I'd be happy to help you explore your interests and hobbies."

"I'm your friend, too," Payson claimed, smirking at him. "After all, how many people would tolerate me pouring water on their head without smacking me."

Unable to help himself, Ishmael snorted as he smiled.

"That's a great look on you, Ish," Madagascar crooned into his ear. "I like hearing you laugh and seeing you happy."

Ishmael smiled up at Madagascar, realizing he liked it, too. Slowly, he sobered as something else Yuma said rose in his mind.

"How do I reconnect with my wolf?"

"Depending on your meds, that could take a little time," Ryan warned while shaking his head. "We just don't know."

A dark-haired man who looked to be in his late forties with steel-gray eyes appeared next to them. "You think you're a wolf shifter?" he asked bluntly, staring at him intently.

Feeling the urge to duck his head, Ishmael did just that as he murmured, "Um, maybe?"

"I'm Diego Tamang, ex-wolf-shifter alpha," the man told him, lowering to one knee next to him. "Vail is my grandson, also a wolf shifter."

"Grandson?" Ishmael gaped at the man. "Wow."

"I'm sure Mads told you we live a few centuries." Chuckling, Diego held out his hand, palm up. "Why don't you come with me, and we'll see if we can't connect with your wolf."

After looking at Madagascar and receiving a reassuring nod, Ishmael took Diego's hand and allowed the other man to help him to his feet.

Chapter Nine

"How's Ishmael doing?" Kontra asked as he settled in a camping chair beside Madagascar's. "He looks happy in his furry form."

Madagascar smiled as he watched Ishmael frolic with not only Vail in wolf form but several other shifters in their furry forms. They were wrestling and tumbling across the lawn. Even though Ishmael's wolf form was just as massive as his human form, he was just as sweet as a canine, too—a gentle giant. Ishmael easily deferred to not only Diego but Vail, too.

Hell, in a real pack, Madagascar would bet that his mate would actually have ended up a fairly submissive wolf. He bet that it was the scientists who'd turned him into such a large animal. While Madagascar loved his wolf's size—he and some of the other bears had joined in the play for a short while, too—he loved his nature even more.

"He really does." Madagascar loved that it had only taken the wolves half a day to coax out Ishmael's animal. He figured it was because he'd already missed a couple of doses of meds coupled with Ishmael already claiming him and Diego's dominant nature. "I'm really happy for him." Frowning, Madagascar admitted, "Those marks on his back sure as hell don't look like burn marks. More like whip marks. I'm almost afraid to talk to him about trying to find out what happened to him."

Kontra cleared his throat as he placed a tablet on his thigh. "Well, I have a little information about that." A muscle ticked in the grizzly shifter's jaw once before he met Madagascar's gaze. "Normally, I'd have Lamar bury any information this traumatic to a psyche, but in this case, there's bits I think Ishmael needs to know."

Madagascar tensed, a frown tugging at his lips. Tightening his hold on his beer bottle, he asked, "What is it?"

After waking the tablet, Kontra showed him a picture. "Ishmael's older brother is looking for him."

Looking at a young man that appeared remarkably similar to Ishmael, with a few extra muscles that didn't seem quite natural, Madagascar let out a long sigh. "He was experimented on, too. Wasn't he?"

Kontra nodded once. "This is Boaz Cartwright. Boaz and Ishmael were part of the Coonie pack, which was decimated in nineteen-eighty-nine." The big male's expression turned sad as he shook his head. "For a long time, it was blamed on these two men." He used a hand to indicate Boaz's picture, followed by a playing Ishmael. "Except, they were both captured and sold to scientists by Krakow, and he framed them."

Madagascar growled low in his throat, knowing Kontra referred to a wolf shifter that had been a councilman. His shady dealings had been brought to light by the Stone Ridge wolf pack. When he'd been removed as councilman, Krakow had gone rogue and had eventually been dispatched.

"They've been cleared now, of course," Kontra continued, relaxing in his seat. "But since Boaz is looking for Ishmael, has been since he was rescued and coaxed back into human form by his mate, I thought we should give Ishmael a chance to reconnect with him."

"Ishmael doesn't remember his family," Madagascar pointed out, hating the idea of offering anything that might hurt his mate, who'd already been through too much abuse.

Kontra shook his head. "Doesn't matter. Boaz does, and he could share some good things with Ishmael." Offering Madagascar an encouraging smile, he told him, "Until the massacre, Boaz has nothing but good memories of his past."

"You said that Boaz was coaxed back to human form by his mate?" Madagascar asked, wondering about that.

With a nod, Kontra explained, "Unlike Ishmael, Boaz's experimentation went a different way. He was given drugs to make him extremely aggressive along with the tweaking of his size." The grizzly shifter frowned as he peered toward the trees. "When they lost control of Boaz, he was tagged for termination, but the Stone Ridge pack got to him first." He grimaced as he admitted, "They had to keep him locked up, too, of a sort, until a chance encounter with his mate helped Boaz break through the block they'd put on his mind."

Nodding, understanding Kontra's reasoning, Madagascar told him, "I'll talk to him." As he watched Ishmael's wolf pounce on the back of a white tiger, he had to admit, "I'm pretty sure he'll want to meet him. He has that kind of soft heart."

"Figured as much just from watching him for a few hours," Kontra declared. Patting his leg, he prepared to rise. "When Ishmael's done playing, bring him—"

"Alpha." Lamar's call interrupted the alpha shifter. The peacock shifter's cheeks were flushed, and he carried another tablet. "Sorry to interrupt. Code Red."

Kontra growled low in his throat as he took the tablet from Lamar. Whatever he saw caused him to roar. The noise was more reminiscent of a bear call—something that should never have been able to come from a human's throat.

Many of the animals playing in the yard scattered, sprinting into the cypress trees ringing them. A few were herding the new arrivals, obviously accepting responsibility for them. Adam's white tiger nosed a cowering Ishmael toward them.

Madagascar hurried toward his mate, Kontra following him. "Don't shift," the alpha ordered, pointing at them both. "You're faster in your four-legged forms." Scowling at his tablet, Kontra grumbled, "And we damn sure don't want them to get their hands on either of you."

Just as Kontra finished speaking, the roar of several engines came from the front of the house.

"Let's see who's decided to drop in," Kontra rumbled, striding toward the corner of the house. Instantly, he was flanked by Beta Sam and Enforcer Mutegi. "Keep a sharp eye, guys."

Indecision filling him, Madagascar glanced toward the trees where he knew the rest of his bear sleuth would be waiting. He rested his hand on Ishmael's shoulder, wondering what his mate would prefer. Would he want to face his tormentors?

Adam bounded away from them. Instead of heading into the trees, he headed for the house. The tiger jumped from the porch railing to the roof, and he began prowling toward the front.

"Where is he, Olson?"

A woman's voice echoed through the still afternoon air. From the way Ishmael whined and pressed against him, Madagascar figured his mate would know. He also knew that Olson had once been a guard at a different facility that Kontra had shut down.

Is that Doctor Meyer? And if so, how does she know Olson? Did she work out of the other facility at some point?

"Who are you talking about, Doctor Meyer?" Olson asked, his deep voice carrying easily to him.

That answers that.

The woman issued a very un-lady-like snort. "Don't toy with me, Olson. I left you alone because I knew you'd quit before my other facility was hit. I'd assumed, wrongly evidently, that you didn't have anything to do with it." Anger began to make her voice rise. "And now, my main facility is wiped out, my shifters taken, and you and your friends have even stolen my pet project. Where is Ishmael? I want him back."

"Why do you want Ishmael?" Kontra's voice filled the air. "How come you're not asking about the others?"

"Who are you?" Meyer demanded.

"Most around these parts call me boss," Kontra replied, lying through his teeth. The only one who called him that was Payson. Evidently, Kontra didn't plan to advertise that he was a shifter. "Olson told me about your illegal activities, so I brought a team to stop you."

"You can't stop us," Meyer declared with a scoff. "You're a shifter, right? You look like one. A big one." Her tone turned calculating. "We've gleaned so much information from studying and experimenting on your kind that I could kill you with a snap of my fingers."

That sounded a little dramatic.

Ishmael growled softly and began stalking around the house. As much as Madagascar wanted to stop him, he knew his mate needed this. Ishmael needed closure on this part of his life in order to properly move on.

Staying close, Madagascar paused at the front corner. A touch to Ishmael's ruff made his mate do the same. They were in sight of the front, after all.

May as well not advertise our presence.

Madagascar took in the four vehicles fanned out before Olson's Victorian home. There was one quad-cab pick-up, two SUVs, and one box truck. It looked like they came prepared to grab more than just Ishmael.

A brunette stood in front of the hood of the pick-up. There were two armed men flanking her. They each had a gun in hand and were pointing it toward the house. A half dozen more men stood near the vehicles, weapons in hand and obviously ready to react to . . . whatever.

"Now, where is—ah, there you are, Ishmael." Doctor Meyer frowned at Ishmael. "While I'm not pleased you shifted, I know I can fix it." Heaving a displeased sigh, she shook her head. "You must have been forgetting your meds.

I thought I'd stopped that thoughtless behavior with the lashings years ago." With a flick of her fingers toward the box truck, Meyer stated, "No matter. I'll get it sorted."

Madagascar twisted his fingers in Ishmael's thick fur, just in case he made a move toward the box truck, but his mate stayed put. Relief filled Madagascar.

"Out of curiosity, why did you keep Ishmael as a human for so long?" Kontra crossed his arms over his massive torso, his comments sounding conversational. "Normally, your kind just terminates our kind when you don't get your experiments right."

Meyer sneered. "I'm not as short-sighted as those other scientists. One hiccup doesn't ruin an experiment I'd spent years working on." She rolled a shoulder negligently. "It just meant I had to put it on hold." Meyer's smile turned sickly sweet as she focused on Ishmael. "I hear they planned to terminate your brother when they messed up the formula they gave him, making him feral, so I didn't use it on you." Smirking, Doctor Meyer's eyes hardened in a cruel expression as she continued to taunt Ishmael. "I decided to tweak the formula in my spare time, but that meant I needed to make you useful until I could sort out the problem. Better than having you lying about a cage, you know. Janitors are always necessary, and a big, dumb shifter whose brain cells had been destroyed by my tests and wouldn't know any better would be perfect for the job." With a laugh, Meyer claimed, "Hell, if all else fails, I could start a cleaning service by duplicating my work on others of your kind. I'd be rich. No one likes cleaning anymore."

Madagascar felt the shudder run through Ishmael's body, and his worst fears were realized. His mate was shifting. The change was slow and sounded a little painful, leaving his big sweet wolf vulnerable.

Meyer laughed as Ishmael changed. "Get them, boys."

Then she lifted her hand and made as if to snap her fingers.

The report of a high-powered rifle filled the air. Blood sprayed from Meyer's hand — which now sported two missing fingers. Screaming in obvious pain, Meyer flailed her good hand, ordering her men to attack.

Knowing Ryan's work when he saw it, Madagascar scoffed as he swung into action.

Can't have her snapping her fingers, after all.

CHAPTER TEN

Having gone so long without shifting, Ishmael knew he was taking too long. He heard the sound of a gun, heard Doctor Meyer's scream, and felt Madagascar's arms around him, but he could do nothing. For several long, agonizing seconds, Ishmael knew he was completely vulnerable.

I should have listened to Kontra. Shifting was a bad idea. I just wanted to ask why so bad . . . and about my brother.

Finally finished, Ishmael blinked quickly, clearing his vision. He realized he'd been tugged around the side of the house. Madagascar stood with his shirt in his hands, holding it out to him.

"Wrap it around your waist," Madagascar ordered.

While Ishmael took it, he couldn't help thinking that his nudity seemed like it should be the least of their worries. After all, weren't there over half a dozen guys with guns around the corner? Except, then Ishmael realized he didn't actually hear the sound of gunfire.

Seeing Madagascar peeking around the corner, Ishmael asked, "What's going on?"

Madagascar scoffed and shook his head. "Come and see." Then he wrapped his arm around Ishmael's waist and urged him forward a couple of steps so he could check out the front yard.

Ishmael's eyes widened as he took in the scene.

Kontra and his friends still stood where they had been, and he actually looked bored. Sam looked annoyed, and Mutegi sported an expression Ishmael couldn't read. Someone had bandaged Doctor Meyer's hand, and she stood red-faced and angry. One of the men with her had his palm up to the air, and he seemed confused. A couple of the other men exchanged glances with fear in their eyes.

"What science is this?" Doctor Meyer yelled, glaring at her men. "Some kind of force field? Short it out! Get me my experiments back, or you'll all be sorry."

Sadness flooded Ishmael, and he knew the *why*. Doctor Meyer saw them as nothing more than property — things to do with as she saw fit. Ishmael realized he was lucky she hadn't disposed of him a long time ago, considering the words she'd spewed earlier.

"Not science. Magick." The melodious tenor filled the clearing as a stunningly pretty man appeared. Appearing about five-foot-ten in height, his long, white hair flowing on the slight breeze, he sauntered forward, every step accentuating his lean runner's build. Even from that distance, Ishmael could make out the disdain the man felt as he stared at Doctor Meyer and her people with vibrant lavender eyes. "Fae magick, to be exact." Tipping his chin up, he peered at them with a haughty expression. "You've come to the wrong place, scientist, and now, it's the last mistake you'll ever make."

"What are you?" one of the men asked, taking a step backward.

"Fae, of course," the man replied, his tone droll. He refocused on the doctor. "Your men seem a bit dim. Guess you didn't hire them for their brains."

"Cease whatever you're doing at once," Doctor Meyer demanded, actually resting her good hand on her hip. "You have no jurisdiction here, fae. Go back to your own realm. This is our business."

The fae tipped his head back and laughed at her audacity.

Ishmael knew he could be a little slow, but even he realized that Doctor Meyer had no say in the situation. He also realized that she evidently had extensive knowledge of the paranormal. Ishmael had never heard of the fae, and he desperately wanted to ask Madagascar about the man as well as what the doctor meant by going back to his realm.

Keeping his mouth shut, Ishmael decided to do it later.

"Thank you, Elron," Kontra rumbled, addressing the fae. "I appreciate the shield."

"My pleasure, Alpha." The fae—Elron—slung his arm around the waist of the muscular, Native American man who'd been flanking him. "If Castor and I are to make this our home after you leave, it's time I take a little more responsibility."

"Yeah. That'll be the day," a man stated with a snort as he appeared as if out of nowhere. He, too, had lavender eyes, but this man was big, broad, and bald. Smirking, the second fae crossed his arms over his chest. "But nice shield."

"Thanks." Elron snickered as he bowed deeply. "And you know me too well, Prudhoe."

Prudhoe sobered as he focused on Kontra. "What do you want done with these assholes?"

Kontra glanced Ishmael's way before sighing deeply. "I'm sorry you have to see paranormal justice so soon after your awakening, Ishmael." He scowled at the group as he continued, "But the atrocities this woman has perpetuated against our kind has only one consequence. Death."

"You can't kill me," Doctor Meyer screamed. "What I did was in the name of science. I helped people."

"By torturing shifters," Sam cut in with a growl. "The ends don't justify the means."

When the doctor opened her mouth again, Kontra interrupted, "But first, we need to know a few things."

Sneering, Doctor Meyer lifted her chin. "I won't tell you abominations a damn thing."

Ishmael flinched, cuddling harder against Madagascar's

side. He hated hearing what she really thought of him. Still, he figured if he hadn't, he would always wonder.

"Ah, there's the slurs," Madagascar muttered, shaking his head. "Knew they'd turn up somewhere."

"Fortunately, we don't need you to tell us anything," Kontra claimed. Turning, he caught the eye of another approaching male. "May I introduce Draven, a warlock and vampire. He'll extract whatever we need from you before we carry out your sentence."

"If you kill me, people will come looking," Doctor Meyer declared, backing up a step as she peered around wildly—not that there was anywhere any of them could go. "You'll never be safe here. Let me go, and I'll never return. We can forget any of this ever happened."

Scoffing, Draven curled his lip, revealing a fang. "As if we'd believe you." He'd paused just outside the shielded area. "You reek of deceit."

Ishmael was tempted to get closer to Doctor Meyer just so he could know what that smelled like. He must have made a move, for he felt Madagascar's arm tighten around him. Focusing on his bear-shifter lover, Ishmael saw his arched brow and knew what it was—a silent question.

Shrugging, Ishmael admitted, "Wanted to know what that smelled like."

"You really don't," Draven countered, peering over his shoulder at him. His blue eyes were narrowed, and his pale lips were curled. "It smells really bad. Worse than rotten eggs."

Even as Ishmael nodded, he figured he would have to ask Madagascar about that later. He didn't remember ever smelling rotten eggs.

"You can't do anything to me with us behind this shield," Doctor Meyer claimed, perhaps still looking for a way out of the mess she'd walked into. "And as soon as it drops, we'll just shoot everyone."

As if to back up her words, the over half a dozen men with her raised their weapons and picked a target.

Doctor Meyer tapped the man next to her and pointed at Ishmael. "Kill him first," she ordered as she glared at him. "If I'm going to die, I want to see him die first. This is all his fault."

Ishmael sucked in a sharp breath upon hearing her words. He tried to press closer to Madagascar's side, but he was already flush against him. A shudder worked through Ishmael, and he was tempted to turn and run back around the side of the house.

Madagascar snarled, stepping in front of him. "Why can't the damn bad guys take responsibility for their own fucking actions?"

Yup. I definitely think it's time to run.

If Ishmael had remained in wolf form, he would have had his tail between his legs.

"Because they are misguided assholes," Mutegi stated dryly, shaking his head. "Always the same."

"Man, boss." Payson sauntered out of the woods, appearing unconcerned with his nudity. Maybe it was a common thing for him. "This is a little anti-climactic. I thought we were gonna fight, but Tim and Evan did some new magick mojo thingy they'd been practicing, and they put all the soldiers creeping through the woods to sleep." Payson scowled, looking clearly disgruntled, and crossed his arms over his chest. "I was lookin' forward to kickin' some butt."

Kontra grinned widely as he chuckled. "Sorry, Payson." He patted the hyena shifter on his back. "You'll have to settle for attacking one of those guys." He pointed. "We're about to drop the shield."

"Sweet!" Payson brightened as he crouched and shifted into his animal.

"Uh, actually, sorry, Payson." Tim appeared from between

a couple of trees. "But I just used a spell to melt their triggers, so now they're all stuck." He lifted his hands in a sorry gesture. "They're all unarmed now." When Payson's hyena drooped, Tim offered, "Maybe they'll be stupid and fight anyway. Or run away, and you'll have to catch them."

Payson lifted his head again, glancing between the men.

Maybe he was trying to figure out if one of them was likely to do that.

Clapping his hands, Kontra stated, "Okay, then." He turned to Ishmael and stated, "Is there anything you want to say to the doc, Ishmael? She wronged you the most." Lifting a hand, palm out, Kontra added the caveat, "Just don't ask for mercy for her because I'd hate to have to deny you."

Ishmael nibbled his bottom lip for a moment, thinking. Eyeing Doctor Meyer, someone he'd looked up to for as far back as his memories stretched, he saw the hatred written all over her face. The woman before him wasn't the same one who he'd spent time with. This woman, he didn't know.

With a sigh, Ishmael asked Kontra, "Do you think Draven would be able to figure out if my brother really is dead?" While Ishmael didn't remember the man, he still wanted to know.

"No need for him to check, Ishmael," Kontra told him with a warm smile. "Boaz is alive and well. A group of us plan to head to the area where he's living now. If you want, we'll take you with us."

"Really?" Ishmael felt anticipation fill him when he saw Kontra nod. "Okay."

Kontra focused on Madagascar and stated, "Mads, why don't you take Ishmael into the house? He doesn't need to be here for what's going to happen next."

Madagascar nodded. "Yes, Alpha." Then he threaded his fingers with Ishmael's and headed for the porch. "Come on, Ish. Let's go get cleaned up, and I'll tell you what I know about your brother."

Ishmael followed, doing his best to ignore Doctor Meyer's screams, slurs, and just plain nasty words.

Once the door closed behind them, muffling her voice, Ishmael asked, "Do you think Boaz will want to see me?" After a second of hesitation, he admitted, "I don't remember him."

"I *know* he'll want to see you," Madagascar told him confidently as they ascended the stairs. "Kontra told me he's been looking for you for a couple of years." Smiling over his shoulder at him, his bear shifter added, "He was rescued a couple of years ago, and as soon as he could shift to human, he started asking about you."

Smiling, Ishmael felt a flutter of warmth in his chest. "That's nice of him."

Madagascar paused outside the bathroom. "Yeah."

Drawing Ishmael into his arms, Madagascar held him close, and the warmth Ishmael had been feeling quickly flowed south. He felt his prick thicken, and the flimsy shirt covering could in no way hide it. Unable to help himself, Ishmael pushed his hips forward, searching for friction on his quickly hardening dick.

"My sexy mate," Madagascar rumbled, nuzzling Ishmael's neck. "Love how you respond to me."

"Love it, too," Ishmael admitted, dipping his head and inhaling Madagascar's scent. With his wolf now having a presence in his mind, he growled upon seeing his mark on Madagascar's neck. Wanting a matching one on his own, Ishmael asked, "Will you bite and claim me, too?"

"Absolutely," Madagascar replied, sliding a hand up to cradle Ishmael's jaw. Meeting his gaze, he told him, "I want to share a shower with you, wash you all over, and take away the stress of the day."

Ishmael immediately began to nod, liking the idea of seeing a wet, naked Madagascar. "Wanna wash you, too."

Running his hands over a soapy Madagascar sounded like so much fun.

Madagascar rumbled softly. "I'd love that, Ish." His dark eyes narrowed as a feral smile curved his lips. "After that, we'll go into our bedroom, and I plan on holding you, loving on you, and when you're ready, I'm going to claim you. Think you can handle that?"

Nodding eagerly, Madagascar could hardly wait. "Yes, please, Mads. All that."

"And we'll never be alone again," Madagascar declared. "You and me against the world."

"And with our family and friends," Ishmael reminded, thinking of all the wonderful new people he'd met . . . and his brother. With those thoughts, he realized something important. "With you and them, I finally have a future. I finally have a life."

"Me, too, Ish," Madagascar replied with a smile. "You gave me a life, too."

Ishmael grinned, liking the sound of that. "Then let's get started."

"Your wish is my command."

Ishmael followed Madagascar into the bathroom, ready for everything his bear mate had promised, happy to follow him anywhere.

To Ishmael's pleasure, Madagascar didn't disappoint.

ABOUT THE AUTHOR

Charlie started writing fantasy when she was eight, and after stumbling onto her first erotic romance at age nineteen, she realized her true calling. She now focuses on writing gay erotic romance, normally of the paranormal variety, with heroes of all kinds. With the help and support of her husband, Charlie finally fulfilled one of her life-long goals . . . move to acreage with her horses. You can often find her curled up with her laptop and a cup of tea or glass of wine, creating her next adventure. Charlie enjoys exploring the mountains of her new Oregon home on horseback, 4-wheeler, or motorcycle.

She can be reached at ch.richards2010@yahoo.com

Or visit her at www.charlie-richards.com.

www.ingramcontent.com/pod-product-compliance
Lightning Source LLC
Chambersburg PA
CBHW070540130626
46555CB00003B/1504